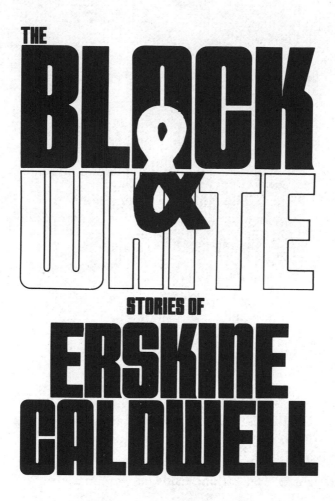

THE BLACK & WHITE STORIES OF ERSKINE CALDWELL

SELECTED BY RAY McIVER • FOREWORD BY ERSKINE CALDWELL

PEACHTREE PUBLISHERS, LTD.

Published by
PEACHTREE PUBLISHERS, LTD.
494 Armour Circle, N.E.
Atlanta, Georgia 30324

Manufactured in the United States of America

First printing

Library of Congress Catalog Number 84-60921

ISBN: 0-931948-63-0

DEDICATION

This book is for my golden grandsons, Kevin and Eric,
Whom I envy even as I dedicate:

They have before them so much more time than I
To read the works of the author of these tales.

CONTENTS

IN THE NATION THAT IS NOT . . .

Candy-Man Beechum 3
Daughter 8
The End of Christy Tucker 14
Saturday Afternoon 21
Kneel to the Rising Sun 28

OURS WERE IDLE PLEASURES . . .

Blue Boy 55
Return to Lavinia 60
August Afternoon 67
The Picture 76
Yellow Girl 83
Picking Cotton 95
Wild Flowers 100

THE MORTAL SICKNESS OF A MIND . . .

The Negro in the Well 111
Runaway 118
The People v. Abe Lathan, Colored 124
Savannah River Payday 133

WHY SHOULD MEN MAKE HASTE TO DIE?

The Fly in the Coffin 143
Big Buck 148
Nine Dollars' Worth of Mumble 159
Meddlesome Jack 166
The Courting of Susie Brown 179
Squire Dindiddy 185

Foreword

Life was often cruel and painful for black and white alike in the Deep South during the beginning and middle decades of our century. The ravages of hunger and want and disease, together with the merciless whiplash of inhumanity, made the ordeal of living a savage heritage for many of both races.

As it happened, and fortunately so for me as a white Southerner and aspiring writer, I came to know and to mingle with many black Southerners at an early age. My first playmate was a chubby-faced mulatto youngster at my birthplace in Georgia. Years later, among muscular workmates on Southern farms there were usually several teen-age black boys. And, once briefly, an elderly Negro was my friendly cellmate in an unsegregated Louisiana jail.

It seems to me now as an author of many years that the short story is the ideal form of fiction to depict the true visage and overt actions of mankind and, most of all, to reveal the inner spirit of the individual. The long and laborious novel can be written with consummate skill and then in the end, usually padded with contrivances, it may amount to little more than a dismal depository of excessive verbiage. However, the short story, in its incisive brevity and purpose, can be intent and able to reveal, with verity and sympathy, the motives and prejudices of its characters in time of joy and sorrow, humor and tragedy.

This collection of short fiction is offered with the thought that some readers will accept parts of it with approval while others will reject portions of it in outrage. Whatever the reaction may be, it is the hope of the author that the spirit of the characters and the essence of the incidents will leave a memorable impression of a kind upon all readers.

—Erskine Caldwell

Introduction

If you are poring over this bold, presumptuous preface before you've read and relished the twenty-two short stories that follow hard upon it, then surely you are polite but most impolitic.

Therefore, so that you may not be restrained any longer than necessary from the feast that waits within, I shall be as brief as woman's love.

In 1941, while loafing in the stacks of the John Hope Library on the campus of Atlanta University, I came upon and read for the first of now uncounted times a very short story by Erskine Caldwell — "The Fly in the Coffin." I knew instantly that this brief, bright tale, if properly dramatized, would suit and stimulate the talents of a cry of players with whom I was consorting at the time.

I produced a drama out of the story, and it was acted out to the seeming joys of the cast and crew of The Community Players; but all this was done without the knowledge or consent, it now must be confessed, of the author.

Fifteen years later, the selfsame players wanted to revive the original production. This time, a maturer conscience urged me to write Mr. Caldwell and ask for permission to mount the show. By return mail (for this man in correspondence is as punctual as a star and as strict as that fell sergeant Death), Caldwell not only bade us go forward with the business but, on a two-cent postcard dated 12-19-56, kindly asked me to send him a copy of the dramatization.

Of course, I did not do so . . . you know how fleet of foot Time is when the minions of Procrastination are having fun. It was not until June of 1961, when The WERD Theatre yearned to do this little classic *scherzo* on radio, that I sent the patient author the piece.

A very few days later, in New York City, I received an incredible letter from Erskine Caldwell directing unworthy and unknown me to choose from among his short stories two that might be adapted for the stage, and to submit them to his literary agent of the moment, James Oliver Brown, in hopes of a Broadway production.

All this was done, but in spite of Caldwell's good wishes, Jim Brown's boundless energies, and a series of carefully composed pagan prayers by me, Broadway soon turned her hunched back on "O Rising Sun!" — the product of our labors.

But, happily for me, out of the venture there came seven pretty good plays and a fixed and valued friendship with a fine fellow.

Sometime later, Mr. Caldwell gave me *carte blanche* to arrange certain of his short stories into a book and further invited me to write an introduction. The result you hold in your hands.

But why, you might ask, do we need another anthology from the works of Erskine Caldwell?

This anthology is unique: it differs widely from others made out of Caldwell's writings. Each tale herein treats with artistic accuracy many and sundry relationships, fixed and forged, between some black people and some white people who lived (and still dwell?) in some Southern towns in America.

There was once a time when to do deeds of dreadful note to certain people was judged good, right, and manful; but to *report* these actions fingered the writer out as Trouble Maker, Outside Agitator, or even Communist. Well, in those perilous-to-many years, Erskine Caldwell wrote what he damned-well pleased, and to hell with those who would harm him if they could.

He wrote of the merry and the oppressed, with especial passion for the black man who came naked into the world, toiled and endured all manner of shame and humiliation in order merely to survive.

From birth to death, this black man lived under THE GREAT FEAR: the fear of doing, saying, thinking the wrong thing at the wrong place, at the wrong time; the great fear of violating certain unique laws of God and White-folks — unwritten ordinances prescribed for him alone. It was a time when the outlandish was the ordinary, when the obscene was the usual.

The souls of some of these unfortunates are in the present stories. Thanks to Erskine Caldwell, they live in perpetuity.

—Ray McIver

In the Nation
That is Not . . .

Candy-Man Beechum

It was ten miles out of the Ogeechee swamps, from the sawmill to the top of the ridge, but it was just one big step to Candy-Man. The way he stepped over those Middle Georgia gullies was a sight to see.

"Where you goin', Candy-Man?"

"Make way for these flapping feet, boy, because I'm going for to see my gal. She's standing on the tips of her toes waiting for me now."

The rabbits lit out for the hollow logs where those stomping big feet couldn't get nowhere near them.

"Don't tread on no white-folks' toes, Candy-Man," Little Bo said. "Because the white-folks is first-come."

Candy-Man Beechum flung a leg over the rail fence just as if it had been a hoe handle to straddle. He stood for a minute astride the fence, looking at the black boy. It was getting dark in the swamps, and he had ten miles to go.

"Me and white-folks don't mix," Candy-Man told him, "just as long as they leave me be. I skin their mules for them, and I snake their cypress logs, but when the day is done, I'm long gone where the white-folks ain't are."

Owls in the trees began to take on life. Those whooing birds were glad to see that setting sun.

The black boy in the mule yard scratched his head and watched the sun go down. If he didn't have all those mules to feed, and if he had had a two-bit piece in his pocket, he'd have liked to tag along with Candy-Man. It was Saturday night, and there'd be a barrelful of catfish frying in town that evening. He wished he had some of that good-smelling cat.

"Before the time ain't long," Litte Bo said, "I'm going to get me myself a gal."

"Just be sure she ain't Candy-Man's, boy, and I'll give you a helping hand."

He flung the other leg over the split-rail fence and struck out for the high land. Ten miles from the swamps to the top of the ridge, and his trip would be done. The bushes whipped around his legs, where his legs had been. He couldn't be waiting for the back-strike of no swamp-country bushes. Up the log road, and across the bottom land, taking three corn rows at a stride, Candy-Man Beechum was on his way.

There were some colored boys taking their time in the big road. He was up on them before they had time to turn their heads around.

"Make way for these flapping feet, boys," he shouted. "Here I come!"

"Where you going, Candy-Man?"

They had to do a lot of running to keep up with him. They had to hustle to match those legs four feet long. He made their breath come short.

"Somebody asked me where I'm going," Candy-Man said. "I got me a yellow gal, and I'm on my way to pay her some attention."

"You'd better toot your horn, Candy-Man, before you open her door. Yellow gals don't like to be taken by surprise."

"Boy, you're tooting the truth, except that you don't know the whyfor of what you're saying. Candy-Man's gal always waits for him right at the door."

"Saturday-night bucks sure have to hustle along. They have to strike pay before the Monday-morning whistle starts whipping their ears."

The boys fell behind, stopping to blow and wheeze. There was no keeping up, on a Saturday night, with the seven-foot mule skinner on his way.

The big road was too crooked and curvy for Candy-Man. He struck out across the fields, headed like a plumb line for a dishful of frying catfish. The lights of the town came up to meet him in the face like a swarm of lightning bugs. Eight miles to town, and two more to go, and he'd be rapping on that yellow gal's door.

Back in the big road, when the big road straightened out, Candy-Man swung into town. The old folks riding, and the young ones walking, they all made way for those flapping feet. The mules to the buggies and the sports in the middle of the road all got aside to let him through.

"What's you big hurry, Candy-Man?"

"Take care my dust don't choke you blind, niggers. I'm on my way."

"Where to, Candy-Man?"

"I got a gal what's waiting right at her door. She don't like for to be kept waiting."

"Better slow down and cool those heels, Candy-Man, because you're coming to the white-folks' town. They don't like niggers stepping on their toes."

"When the sun goes down, I'm on my own. I can't be stopping to see what color people be."

The old folks clucked, and the mules began to trot. They didn't like the way that big coon talked.

"How about taking me along, Candy-Man?" the young bucks begged. "I'd like to grab me a chicken off a hen-house roost."

"Where I'm going I'm the cock of the walk. I gouge my spurs in all strange feathers. Stay away, black boy, stay away."

Down the street he went, sticking to the middle of the road. The sidewalks couldn't hold him when he was in a hurry like that. A plateful of frying catfish, and he would be on his way. That yellow gal was waiting, and there was no time to lose. Eight miles covered, and two short ones to go. That sawmill fireman would have to pull on that Monday-morning whistle like it was the rope to the promised land.

The smell of the fish took him straight to the fish-house door. Maybe they were mullets, but they smelled just as good. There wasn't enough time to order up a special dish of fins.

He had his hand on the restaurant door. When he had his supper, he would be on his way. He could see that yellow gal waiting for him only a couple of miles away.

All those boys were sitting at their meal. The room was full of hungry people just like him. The stove was full of frying fish, and the barrel was only halfway used. There was enough good eating for a hundred hungry men.

He still had his hand on the fish-house door, and his nose was soaking it in. If he could have his way about it, some of these days he was going to buy himself a whole big barrel of catfish and eat them every one.

"What's your hurry, Candy-Man?"

"No time to waste, white-boss. Just let me be."

The night policeman snapped open the handcuffs, and reached for his arms. Candy-Man stepped away.

"I reckon I'd better lock you up. It'll save a lot of trouble. I'm getting good and tired of chasing fighting niggers all over town every Saturday night."

"I never hurt a body in all my life, white-boss. And I sure don't pick fights. You must have the wrong nigger, white-boss. You sure has got me wrong. I'm just passing through for to see my gal."

"I reckon I'll play safe and lock you up till Monday morning just the same. Reach out your hands for these cuffs, nigger."

Candy-Man stepped away. His yellow gal was on his mind. He didn't feel like passing her up for no iron-bar jail. He stepped away.

"I'll shoot you down, nigger. One more step, and I'll blast away."

"White-boss, please just let me be. I won't even stop to get my supper, and I'll shake my legs right out of town. Because I just got to see my gal before the Monday-morning sun comes up."

Candy-Man stepped away. The night policeman threw down the handcuffs and jerked out his gun. He pulled the trigger at Candy-Man, and Candy-Man fell down.

"There wasn't no cause for that, white-boss. I'm just a big black nigger with itching feet. I'd a heap rather be traveling than standing still."

The people came running, but some of them turned around and went the other way. Some stood and looked at Candy-Man while he felt his legs to see if they could hold him up. He still had two miles to go before he could reach the top of the ridge.

The people crowded around, and the night policeman put away his gun. Candy-Man tried to get up so he could be getting on down the road. That yellow gal of his was waiting for him at her door, straining on the tips of her toes.

"White-boss, I sure am sorry you had to go and shoot me down. I never bothered white-folks, and they sure oughtn't bother me. But there ain't much use in living if that's the way it's going to be. I reckon I'll just have to blow out the light and fade away. Just reach me a blanket so I can cover my skin and bones."

"Shut up, nigger," the white-boss said. "If you keep on talking with that big mouth of yours, I'll just have to pull out my gun again and hurry you on."

The people drew back to where they wouldn't be standing too close. The night policeman put his hand on the butt of his gun, where it would be handy, in case.

"If that's the way it's to be, then make way for Candy-Man Beechum, because here I come."

(First published in 1935 in *Esquire*)

Daughter

At sunrise a Negro on his way to the big house to feed the mules had taken the word to Colonel Henry Maxwell, and Colonel Henry phoned the sheriff. The sheriff had hustled Jim into town and locked him up in the jail, and then he went home and ate breakfast.

Jim walked around the empty cellroom while he was buttoning his shirt, and after that he sat down on the bunk and tied his shoelaces. Everything that morning had taken place so quickly that he had not even had time to get a drink of water. He got up and went to the water bucket near the door, but the sheriff had forgotten to put water into it.

By that time there were several men standing in the jailyard. Jim went to the window and looked out when he heard them talking. Just then another automobile drove up, and six or seven men got out. Other men were coming towards the jail from both directions of the street.

"What was the trouble out at your place this morning, Jim?"

somebody said.

Jim stuck his chin between the bars and looked at the faces in the crowd. He knew everyone there.

While he was trying to figure out how everybody in town had heard about his being there, somebody else spoke to him.

"It must have been an accident, wasn't it, Jim?"

A colored boy hauling a load of cotton to the gin drove up the street. When the wagon got in front of the jail, the boy whipped up the mules with the ends of the reins and made them trot.

"I hate to see the State have a grudge against you, Jim," somebody said.

The sheriff came down the street swinging a tin dinner pail in his hand. He pushed through the crowd, unlocked the door, and set the pail inside.

Several men came up behind the sheriff and looked over his shoulder into the jail.

"Here's your breakfast my wife fixed up for you, Jim. You'd better eat a little, Jim boy."

Jim looked at the pail, at the sheriff, at the open jail door, and he shook his head.

"I don't feel hungry," he said. "Daughter's been hungry, though — awful hungry."

The sheriff backed out the door, his hand going to the handle of his pistol. He backed out so quickly that he stepped on the toes of the men behind him.

"Now, don't you get careless, Jim boy," he said. "Just sit and calm yourself."

He shut the door and locked it. After he had gone a few steps towards the street, he stopped and looked into the chamber of his pistol to make sure it had been loaded.

The crowd outside the window pressed in closer. Some of the men rapped on the bars until Jim came and look out. When he saw them, he stuck his chin between the iron and gripped his hands around it.

"How come it to happen, Jim?" somebody asked. "It must have been an accident, wasn't it?"

Jim's long thin face looked as if it would come through the bars. The sheriff came up to the window to see if everything was all right.

"Now, just take it easy, Jim boy," he said.

The man who had asked Jim to tell what had happened elbowed the sheriff out of the way. The other men crowded closer.

"How come, Jim?" the man said. "Was it an accident?"

"No," Jim said, his fingers twisting about the bars. "I picked up my shotgun and done it."

The sheriff pushed towards the window again.

"Go on, Jim, and tell us what it's all about."

Jim's face squeezed between the bars until it looked as though only his ears kept his head from coming through.

"Daughter said she was hungry, and I just couldn't stand it no longer. I just couldn't stand to hear her say it."

"Don't get all excited now, Jim boy," the sheriff said, pushing forward one moment and being elbowed away the next.

"She waked up in the middle of the night again and said she was hungry. I just couldn't stand to hear her say it."

Somebody pushed all the way through the crowd until he got to the window.

"Why, Jim, you could have come and asked me for something for her to eat, and you know I'd have given you all I got in the world."

The sheriff pushed forward once more.

"That wasn't the right thing to do," Jim said. "I've been working all year and I made enough for all of us to eat."

He stopped and looked down into the faces on the other side of the bars.

"I made enough working on shares, but they came and took it all away from me. I couldn't go around begging after I'd made enough to keep us. They just came and took it all off. Then Daughter woke up again this morning saying she was hungry, and I just couldn't stand it no longer."

"You'd better go and get on the bunk now, Jim boy," the sheriff said.

"It don't seem right that the little girl ought to be shot like that," somebody said.

"Daughter said she was hungry," Jim said. "She'd been saying that for all of the past month. Daughter'd wake up in the middle of the night and say it. I just couldn't stand it no longer."

"You ought to have sent her over to my house, Jim. Me and my wife could have fed her something, somehow. It don't look right to kill a little girl like her."

"I'd made enough for all of us," Jim said. "I just couldn't stand it no longer. Daughter'd been hungry all the past month."

"Take it easy, Jim boy," the sheriff said, trying to push forward.

The crowd swayed from side to side.

"And so you just picked up the gun this morning and shot her?" somebody asked.

"When she woke up this morning saying she was hungry, I just couldn't stand it."

The crowd pushed closer. Men were coming towards the jail from all directions, and those who were then arriving pushed forward to hear what Jim had to say.

"The State has got a grudge against you now, Jim," somebody said, "but somehow it don't seem right."

"I can't help it," Jim said. "Daughter woke up again this morning that way."

The jailyard, the street, and the vacant lot on the other side were filled with men and boys. All of them were pushing forward to hear Jim. Word had spread all over town by that time that Jim Carlisle had shot and killed his eight-year-old daughter, Clara.

"Who does Jim sharecrop for?" somebody asked.

"Colonel Henry Maxwell," a man in the crowd said. "Colonel Henry has had Jim out there about nine or ten years."

"Henry Maxwell didn't have no business coming and taking all the shares. He's got plenty of his own. It ain't right for Henry Maxwell to come and take Jim's, too."

The sheriff was pushing forward once more.

"The State's got a grudge against Jim now," somebody said. "Somehow it don't seem right, though."

The sheriff pushed his shoulder into the crowd of men and worked his way in closer.

A man shoved the sheriff away.

"Why did Henry Maxwell come and take your share of the crop, Jim?"

"He said I owed it to him because one of his mules died about a month ago."

The sheriff got in front of the barred window.

"You ought to go to the bunk now and rest some, Jim boy," he said. "Take off your shoes and stretch out, Jim boy."

He was elbowed out of the way.

"You didn't kill the mule, did you, Jim?"

"The mule dropped dead in the barn," Jim said. "I wasn't nowhere around. It just dropped dead."

The crowd was pushing harder. The men in front were jammed against the jail, and the men behind were trying to get within earshot. Those in the middle were squeezed against each other so tightly they could not move in any direction. Everyone was talking louder.

Jim's face pressed between the bars and his fingers gripped the iron until the knuckles were white.

The milling crowd was moving across the street to the vacant lot. Somebody was shouting. He climbed up on an automobile and began swearing at the top of his lungs.

A man in the middle of the crowd pushed his way out and went to his automobile. He got in and drove off alone.

Jim stood holding to the bars and looking through the window. The sheriff had his back to the crowd, and he was saying something to Jim. Jim did not hear what he said.

A man on his way to the gin with a load of cotton stopped to find out what the trouble was. He looked at the crowd in the vacant lot for a moment, and then he turned around and looked at Jim behind the bars. The shouting across the street was growing louder.

"What's the trouble, Jim?"

Somebody on the other side of the street came to the wagon. He put his foot on a spoke in the wagon wheel and looked up at the man on the cotton while he talked.

"Daughter woke up this morning again saying she was hungry," Jim said.

The sheriff was the only person who heard him.

The man on the load of cotton jumped to the ground, tied the reins to the wagon wheel, and pushed through the crowd to the car where all the shouting and swearing was being done. After listening for a while, he came back to the street, called a Negro who was standing with several other Negroes on the corner, and handed him the reins. The Negro drove off with the cotton towards the gin, and the man went back into the crowd.

Just then the man who had driven off alone in his car came back. He sat for a moment behind the steering wheel, and then he jumped to the ground. He opened the rear door and took out a crowbar that was as long as he was tall.

"Pry that jail door open and let Jim out," somebody said. "It ain't right for him to be in there."

The crowd in the vacant lot was moving again. The man who had been standing on top of the automobile jumped to the ground, and the men moved towards the street in the direction of the jail.

The first man to reach it jerked the six-foot crowbar out of the soft earth where it had been jabbed.

The sheriff backed off.

"Now, take it easy, Jim boy," he said.

He turned and started walking rapidly up the street towards his house.

(First published in 1933 in *Anvil*)

The End of Christy Tucker

Christy Tucker rode into the plantation town on muleback late in the afternoon, whistling all the way. He had been hewing new pickets for the fence around his house all morning, and he was feeling good for having got so much done. He did not have a chance to go to the plantation town very often, and when he could go he did not lose any time in getting there.

He tied up the mule at the racks behind the row of stores, and the first thing he noticed was the way the other Negroes out there did not seem anxious to speak to him. Christy had been on friendly terms with all the colored people on the plantation ever since he and his wife had moved there three months before, and he could not understand why they pretended not to see him.

He walked slowly down the road toward the plantation office wondering why nobody spoke to him.

After he had gone a little farther, he met Froggy Miller. He caught Froggy by the arm before Froggy could dodge him.

"What's the matter with you folks today?" he said. Froggy Miller lived only a mile from his house in a straight line across the cotton field, and he knew Froggy better than anyone else on the plantation. "What's the matter, anyway, Froggy?"

Froggy, a big six-foot Negro with close-cropped hair, moved away.

He grabbed Froggy by the arm and shook him.

"Now look here!" Christy said, getting worried. "Why do you and everybody else act so strange?"

"Mr. Lee Crossman sent for you, didn't he?" Froggy said.

"Sure, he sent for me," Christy said. "I reckon he wants to talk to me about the farming. But what's that got to do with —"

Before he could finish, Froggy had pulled away from him and walked hurriedly up the road.

Without wasting any more time, Christy ran toward the plantation office to find out what the trouble was.

The plantation bookkeeper, Hendricks, and Lee Crossman's younger brother, Morgan, were sitting in the front office with their feet on the window sill when he ran inside. Hendricks got up when he saw Christy and went through the door into the back room. While the bookkeeper was in the other room, Morgan Crossman stared sullenly at the Negro.

"Come here, you," Hendricks said, coming through the door.

Christy turned around and saw Lee Crossman, the owner and boss of the plantation, standing in the doorway.

"Yes, sir," Christy said.

Lee Crossman was dressed in heavy gray riding breeches and tan shirt, and he wore black boots that laced to his knees. He stood aside while Christy walked into the back room, and closed the door on the outside. Christy walked to the middle of the room and stood there waiting for Lee Crossman.

Christy had moved to the Crossman plantation the first of the year, about three months before. It was the first time he had ever been in Georgia, and he had grown to like it better than Alabama, where he had always lived. He and his wife had decided to come to Georgia because they had heard that the land there was better for sharecropping cotton. Christy said he could not be satisfied merely making a living; he wanted to get ahead in life.

Lee Crossman still had not come, and Christy sat down in one of the chairs. He had no more than seated himself when the door opened. He jumped to his feet.

"Howdy, Mr. Lee," he said, smiling. "I've had a good chance to look at the land, and I'd like to be furnished with another mule and a gang plow. I figure I can raise twice as much cotton on that kind of land with a gang plow, because it's about the best I ever saw. There's not a rock or stump on it, and it's as clear of bushes as the palm of my hand. I haven't even found a gully anywhere on it. If you'll furnish me with another mule and a gang plow, I'll raise more cotton for you than any two sharecroppers on your plantation."

Lee Crossman listened until he had finished, and then he slammed the door shut and strode across the room.

"I sent for you, nigger," he said. "You didn't send for me, did you?"

"That's right, Mr. Lee," he said. "You sent for me."

"Then keep your black face shut until I tell you to open it."

"Yes, sir, Mr. Lee," Christy said, backing across the room until he found himself against the wall. Lee Crossman sat down in a chair and glared at him. "Yes, sir, Mr. Lee," Christy said again.

"You're one of these biggity niggers, ain't you?" Lee said. "Where'd you come from, anyway? You ain't a Georgia nigger, are you?"

"No, sir, Mr. Lee," Christy said, shaking his head. "I was born and raised in Alabama."

"Didn't they teach you any better than this in Alabama?"

"Yes, sir, Mr. Lee."

"Then why did you come over here to Georgia and start acting so biggity?"

"I don't know, Mr. Lee."

Christy wiped his face with the palm of his hand and wondered what Lee Crossman was angry with him about. He began to understand why the other Negroes had gone out of their way to keep from talking to him. They knew he had been sent for, and that meant he had done something to displease Lee Crossman. They did not wish to be seen talking to anyone who was in disfavor with the plantation owner and boss.

"Have you got a radio?" Lee asked.

"Yes, sir."

"Where'd you get it?"

"I bought it on time."

"Where'd you get the money to pay on it?"

"I had a little, and my wife raises a few chickens."

"Why didn't you buy it at the plantation store?"

"I made a better bargain at the other place. I got it a little cheaper."

"Niggers who live on my plantation buy what they need at my plantation store," Lee said.

"I didn't want to go into debt to you, Mr. Lee," Christy said. "I wanted to come out ahead when the accounts are settled at the end of the year."

Lee Crossman leaned back in the chair, crossed his legs, and took out his pocketknife. He began cleaning his fingernails.

There was silence in the room for several minutes. Christy leaned against the wall.

"Stand up straight, nigger!" Lee shouted at him.

"Yes, sir," Christy said, jumping erect.

"Did you split up some of my wood to hew pickets for the fence around the house where you live?"

"Yes, sir, Mr. Lee."

"Why didn't you ask me if I wanted you to do it?"

"I figured the fence needed some new pickets to take the place of some that had rotted, and because I'm living in the house I went ahead and did it."

"You act mighty big, don't you?" Lee said. "You act like you own my house and land, don't you? You act like you think you're as good as a white man, don't you?"

"No sir, Mr. Lee," Christy protested. "I don't try to act any of those ways. I just naturally like to hustle and get things done, that's all. I just can't be satisfied unless I'm fixing a fence or cutting wood or picking cotton, or something. I just naturally like to get things done."

"Do you know what we do with biggity niggers like you in Georgia?"

"No, sir."

"We teach them to mind their own business and stay in their

place."

Lee Crossman got up and crossed the room to the closet. He jerked the door opened and reached inside. When he turned around, he was holding a long leather strap studded with heavy brass brads. He came back across the room, slapping the strap around his boot tops.

"Who told your wife she could raise chickens on my plantation?" he said to Christy.

"Nobody told her, Mr. Lee," Christy said. "We didn't think you'd mind. There's plenty of yard around the house for them, and I built a little hen house."

"Stop arguing with me, nigger!"

"Yes, sir."

"I don't want chickens scratching up crops on this plantation."

"Yes, sir," Christy said.

"Where did you get money to pay on a radio?"

"I snared a few rabbits and skinned them, and then I sold their hides for a little money."

"I don't want no rabbits touched on my plantation," Lee said.

He shook out the heavy strap and cracked it against his boots.

"Why haven't you got anything down on the books in the plantation store?" Lee asked.

"I just don't like to go into debt," Christy said. "I want to come out ahead when the accounts are settled at the end of the year."

"That's my business whether you come out owing or owed at the end of the year," Lee said.

He pointed to a crack in the floor.

"Take off that shirt and drop your pants and get down on your knees astraddle that crack," the white man said.

"What are you going to do to me, Mr. Lee?"

"I'll show you what I'm going to do," he replied. "Take off that shirt and pants and get down there like I told you."

"Mr. Lee, I can't let you beat me like that. No, sir, Mr. Lee. I can't let you do that to me. I just can't!"

"You black-skinned, back-talking coon, you!" Lee shouted, his face turning crimson with anger.

He struck Christy with the heavy, brass-studded strap. Christy backed out of reach, and when Lee struck him the second time, the Negro caught the strap and held on to it. Lee glared at him at first, and then he tried to jerk it out of his grip.

"Mr. Lee, I haven't done anything except catch a few rabbits and raise a few chickens and things like that," Christy protested. "I didn't mean any harm at all. I thought you'd be pleased if I put some new pickets in your fence."

"Shut your mouth and get that shirt and pants off like I told you," he said, angrier than ever. "And turn that strap loose before I blast it loose from you."

Christy stayed where he was and held on to the strap with all his might. Lee was so angry he could not speak after that. He ran to the closet and got his pistol. He swung around and fired it at Christy three times. Christy released his grip on the strap and sank to the floor.

Lee's brother, Morgan, and the bookkeeper, Hendricks, came running into the back room.

"What happened, Lee?" his brother asked, seeing Christy Tucker lying on the floor.

"That nigger threatened me," Lee said, blowing hard. He walked to the closet and tossed the pistol on the shelf.

"You and Hendricks heard him threaten to kill me. I had to shoot him down to protect my own life."

They left the back room and went into the front office. Several clerks from the plantation store ran in and wanted to know what all the shooting was about.

"Just a biggity nigger," Lee said, washing his hands at the sink. "He was that Alabama nigger that came over here two or three months ago. I sent for him this morning to ask him what he meant by putting new pickets in the fence around his house without asking me first. When I got him in here, he threatened me. He was a bad nigger."

The clerks went back to the plantation store, and Hendricks opened up his books and went to work on the accounts.

"Open up the back door," Lee told his brother, "and let those niggers out in the back see what happens when one of them gets as biggity as that coon from Alabama got."

His brother opened the back door. When he looked outside into the road, there was not a Negro in sight. The only living thing out there was the mule on which Christy Tucker had ridden to town.

(First published in 1940 in *The Nation*)

Saturday Afternoon

Tom Denny shoved the hunk of meat out of his way and stretched out on the meat block. He wanted to lie on his back and rest. The meat block was the only comfortable place in the butcher shop where a man could stretch out and Tom just had to rest every once in a while. He could prop his foot on the edge of the block, swing the other leg across his knee and be fairly comfortable with a hunk of rump steak under his head. The meat was nice and cool just after it came from the icehouse. Tom did that. He wanted to rest himself a while and he had to be comfortable on the meat block. He kicked off his shoes so he could wiggle his toes.

Tom's butcher shop did not have a very pleasant smell. Strangers who went in to buy Tom's meat for the first time were always asking him what it was that had died between the walls. The smell got worse and worse year after year.

Tom bit off a chew of tobacco and made himself comfortable on the meat block.

There was a swarm of flies buzzing around the place; those lazy, stinging, fat and greasy flies that lived in Tom's butcher shop. A screen door at the front kept out some of them that tried to get inside, but if they were used to coming in and filling up on the fresh blood on the meat block they knew how to fly around to the back door where there had never been a screen.

Everybody ate Tom's meat, and liked it. There was no other butcher shop in town. You walked in and said, "Hello, Tom. How's everything today?" "Everything's slick as a whistle with me, but my old woman's got the chills and fever again." Then after Tom had finished telling how it felt to have chills and fever, you said, "I want a pound of pork chops, Tom." And Tom said, "By gosh, I'll git it for you right away." While you stood around waiting for the chops Tom turned the hunk of beef over two or three times businesslike and hacked off a pound of pork for you. If you wanted veal it was all the same to Tom. He slammed the hunk of beef around several times making a great to-do, and got the veal for you. He pleased everybody. Ask Tom for any kind of meat you could name, and Tom had it right there on the meat block waiting to be cut off and weighed.

Tom brushed the flies off his face and took a little snooze. It was midday. The country people had not yet got to town. It was laying-by season and everybody was working right up to twelve o'clock sun time, which was half an hour slower than railroad time. There was hardly anybody in town at this time of day, even though it was Saturday. All the town people who had wanted some of Tom's meat for Saturday dinner had already got what they needed, and it was too early in the day to buy Sunday meat. The best time of day to get meat from Tom if it was to be kept over until Sunday was about ten o'clock Saturday night. Then you could take it home and be fairly certain that it would not turn bad before noon the next day — if the weather was not too hot.

The flies buzzed and lit on Tom's mouth and nose and Tom knocked them away with his hand and tried to sleep on the meat block with the cool hunk of rump steak under his head. The tobacco juice kept trying to trickle down his throat and Tom had to keep spitting it out. There was a cigar box half full of sawdust in the corner behind the showcase where livers and brains were kept for display, but he could not quite spit that far from the position he was in. The tobacco juice splattered on the floor midway between the meat block and cigar box. What little of it dripped on the piece of rump steak did not really matter: most people cleaned their meat before they cooked and ate it, and it would all wash off.

But the danged flies! They kept on buzzing and stinging as mean as ever, and there is nothing any meaner than a lazy, well-fed, butcher-shop fly in the summertime, anyway, Tom knocked them off his face and spat them off his mouth the best he could without having to move too much. After a while he let them alone.

Tom was enjoying a good little snooze when Jim Baxter came running through the back door from the barbershop on the corner. Jim was Tom's partner and he came in sometimes on busy days to help out. He was a great big man, almost twice as large as Tom. He always wore a big wide-brimmed black hat and a blue shirt with the sleeves rolled up above his elbows. He had a large egg-shaped belly over which his breeches were always slipping down. When he walked he tugged at his breeches all the time, pulling them up over the top of his belly. But they were always working down until it looked as if they were ready to drop to the ground any minute and trip him. Jim would not wear suspenders. A belt was more sporty-looking.

Tom was snoozing away when Jim ran in the back door and grabbed him by the shoulders. A big handful of flies had gone to sleep on Tom's mouth. Jim shooed them off.

"Hey, Tom, Tom!" Jim shouted breathlessly. "Wake up, Tom! Wake up quick!"

Tom jumped to the floor and pulled on his shoes. He had become so accustomed to people coming in and waking him up to buy a quarter's worth of steak or a quarter's worth of ham that he had mistaken Jim for a customer. He rubbed the back of his hands over his mouth to take away the fly stings.

"What the hell!" he sputtered, looking up and seeing Jim standing there beside him. "What you want?"

"Come on, Tom! Get your gun! We're going after a nigger down the creek a ways."

"God Almighty, Jim!" Tom shouted, now fully awake. He clutched Jim's arm and begged: "You going to git a nigger, sure enough?"

"You're damn right, Tom. You know that gingerbread nigger what used to work on the railroad a long time back? Him's the nigger we're going to git. And we're going to git him good and proper, the yellow-face coon. He said something to Fred Jackson's oldest gal down the road yonder about an hour ago. Fred told us all about it over at the barbershop. Come on, Tom. We got to hurry. I expect we'll jerk him up pretty soon now."

Tom tied on his shoes and ran across the street behind Jim. Tom had his shotgun under his arm, and Jim had pulled the cleaver out of the meat block. They'd get the God-damn nigger all right — God damn his yellow hide to hell!

Tom climbed into an automobile with some other men. Jim jumped on the running board of another car just as it was leaving. There were thirty or forty cars headed for the creek bottom already and more getting ready to start.

They had a place already picked out at the creek. There was a clearing in the woods by the road and there was just enough room to do the job like it should be done. Plenty of dry brushwood nearby and a good-sized sweetgum tree in the middle of the clearing. The automobiles stopped and the men jumped out in a hurry. Some others had gone for Will Maxie. Will was the gingerbread Negro. They would probably find him at home laying his cotton by. Will could grow good cotton. He cut out all the grass first, and then he banked his rows with earth. Everybody else laid his cotton by without going to the trouble of taking out the grass. But Will was a pretty smart Negro. And he could raise a lot of corn too, to the acre. He always cut out the grass before he laid his corn by. But nobody liked Will. He made too much money by taking out the grass before laying by his cotton and corn. He made more money than Tom and Jim made in the butcher shop selling people meat.

Doc Cromer had sent his boy down from the drugstore with half a dozen cases of Coca-Cola and a piece of ice in a wash tub. The tub had some muddy water put in it from the creek, then the chunk of ice, and then three cases of Coca-Cola. When they were gone the boy would put the other three cases in the tub and give the dopes a chance to cool. Everybody likes to drink a lot of dopes when they are nice and cold.

Tom went out in the woods to take a drink of corn with Jim and Hubert Wells. Hubert always carried a jug of corn with him where he happened to be going. He made the whisky himself at his own still and got a fairly good living by selling it around the courthouse and the barbershop. Hubert made the best corn in the county.

Will Maxie was coming up the big road in a hurry. A couple of dozen men were behind him poking him with sticks. Will was getting old. He had a wife and three grown daughters, all married and settled. Will was a pretty good Negro too, minding his own business, stepping out of the road when he met a white man, and otherwise behaving himself. But nobody liked Will. He made too much money by taking the grass out of his cotton before it was laid by.

Will came running up the road and the men steered him into the clearing. It was all fixed. There was a big pile of brushwood and a trace chain for his neck and one for his feet. That would hold him. There were two or three cans of gasoline, too.

Doc Cromer's boy was doing a good business with his Coca-Colas. Only five or six bottles of the first three cases were left in the wash tub. He was getting ready to put the other cases in now and give the dopes a chance to get nice and cool. Everybody likes to have a dope every once in a while.

The Cromer boy would probably sell out and have to go back to town and bring back several more cases. And yet there was not such a big crowd today, either. It was the hot weather that made people have to drink a lot of dopes to stay cool. There were only a hundred and fifty or seventy-five there today. There had not been enough time for the word to get passed around. Tom would have missed it if Jim had not run in and told him about it while he was taking a nap on the meat block.

Will Maxie did not drink Coca-Cola. Will never spent his money on anything like that. That was what was wrong with him. He was too damn good for a Negro. He did not drink corn whisky, nor make it; he did not carry a knife, nor a razor; he bared his head when he met a white man, and he lived with his own wife. But they had him now! God damn his gingerbread hide to hell! They had him where he could not take any more grass out of his cotton before laying it by. They had him tied to a sweet-gum tree in the clearing at the creek with a trace chain around his neck and another around his knees. Yes, sir, they had Will Maxie now, the yellow-face coon! He would not take any more grass out of his cotton before laying it by!

Tom was feeling good. Hubert gave him another drink in the woods. Hubert was all right. He made good corn whisky. Tom liked him for that. And Hubert always took his wife a big piece of meat Saturday night to use over Sunday. Nice meat, too. Tom cut off the meat and Hubert took it home and made a present of it to his wife.

Will Maxie was going up in smoke. When he was just about gone they gave him the lead. Tom stood back and took good aim and fired away at Will with his shotgun as fast as he could breech it and put in a new load. About forty or more of the other men had shotguns too. They filled him so full of lead that his body sagged from his neck where the trace chain held him up.

The Cromer boy had sold completely out. All of his ice and dopes were gone. Doc Cromer would feel pretty good when his boy brought back all that money. Six whole cases he sold, at a dime a bottle. If he had brought along another case or two he could have sold them easily enough. Everybody likes Coca-Cola. There is nothing better to drink on a hot day, if the dopes are nice and cool.

After a while the men got ready to draw the body up in the tree and tie it to a limb so it could hang there, but Tom and Jim could not wait and they went back to town the first chance they got to ride. They were in a big hurry. They had been gone several hours and it was almost four o'clock. A lot of people come downtown early Saturday afternoon to get their Sunday meat before it was picked over by the country people. Tom and Jim had to hurry back and open up the meat market and get to work slicing steaks and chopping soupbones with the cleaver on the meat block. Tom was the butcher. He did all the work with the meat. He went out and killed a cow and quartered her. Then he hauled the meat to the butcher shop and hung it on the hooks in the icehouse. When somebody wanted to buy some meat, he took one of the quarters from the hook and threw it on the meat block and cut what you asked for. You told Tom what you wanted and he gave it to you, no matter what it was you asked for.

Then you stepped over to the counter and paid Jim the money for it. Jim was the cashier. He did all the talking, too. Tom had to do the cutting and weighing. Jim's egg-shaped belly was too big for him to work around the meat block. It got in his way when he tried to slice you a piece of tenderloin steak, so Tom did that and Jim took the money and put it into the cashbox under the counter.

Tom and Jim got back to town just in time. There was a big crowd standing around on the street getting ready to do their weekly trading, and they had to have some meat. You went in the butcher shop and said, "Hello, Tom. I want two pounds and a half of pork chops." Tom said, "Hello, I'll get it for you right away." While you were waiting for Tom to cut the meat off the hunk of rump steak you asked him how was everything.

"Everything's slick as a whistle," he said, "except my old woman's got the chills and fever pretty bad again."

Tom weighed the pork chops and wrapped them up for you and then you stepped over to Jim and paid him the money. Jim was the cashier. His egg-shaped belly was too big for him to work around the meat block. Tom did that part, and Jim took the money and put it into the cashbox under the counter.

(First published in 1930 in *Nativity*)

Kneel to the Rising Sun

A shiver went through Lonnie. He drew his hand away from his sharp chin, remembering what Clem had said. It made him feel now as if he were committing a crime by standing in Arch Gunnard's presence and allowing his face to be seen.

He and Clem had been walking up the road together that afternoon on their way to the filling station when he told Clem how much he needed rations. Clem stopped a moment to kick a rock out of the road, and said that if you worked for Arch Gunnard long enough, your face would be sharp enough to split the boards for your own coffin.

As Lonnie turned away to sit down on an empty box beside the gasoline pump, he could not help wishing that he could be as unafraid of Arch Gunnard as Clem was. Even if Clem was a Negro, he never hesitated to ask for rations when he needed something to eat; and when he and his family did not get enough, Clem came right out and told Arch so. Arch stood for that, but he swore that he was going to run Clem out of the country the first chance he got.

Lonnie knew without turning around that Clem was standing at the corner of the filling station with two or three other Negroes and looking at him, but for some reason he was unable to meet Clem's eyes.

Arch Gunnard was sitting in the sun, honing his jackknife blade on his boot top. He glanced once or twice at Lonnie's hound, Nancy, who was lying in the middle of the road waiting for Lonnie to go home.

"That your dog, Lonnie?"

Jumping with fear, Lonnie's hand went to his chin to hide the lean face that would accuse Arch of short-rationing.

Arch snapped his fingers and the hound stood up, wagging her tail. She waited to be called.

"Mr. Arch, I —"

Arch called the dog. She began crawling towards them on her belly, wagging her tail a little faster each time Arch's fingers snapped. When she was several feet away, she turned over on her back and lay on the ground with her four paws in the air.

Dudley Smith and Jim Weaver, who were lounging around the filling station, laughed. They had been leaning against the side of the building, but they straightened up to see what Arch was up to.

Arch spat some more tobacco juice on his boot top and whetted the jackknife blade some more.

"What kind of a hound dog is that, anyway, Lonnie?" Arch said. "Looks like to me it might be a ketch hound."

Lonnie could feel Clem Henry's eyes boring into the back of his head. He wondered what Clem would do if it had been his dog Arch Gunnard was snapping his fingers at and calling like that.

"His tail's way too long for a coon hound or a bird dog, ain't it, Arch?" somebody behind Lonnie said, laughing out loud.

Everybody laughed then, including Arch. They looked at Lonnie, waiting to hear what he was going to say to Arch.

"Is he a ketch hound, Lonnie?" Arch said, snapping his finger again.

"Mr. Arch, I —"

"Don't be ashamed of him, Lonnie, if he don't show signs of turning out to be a bird dog or a foxhound. Everybody needs a hound around the house that can go out and catch pigs and rabbits when you are in a hurry for them. A ketch hound is a mighty respectable animal. I've known the time when I was mighty proud to own one."

Everybody laughed.

Arch Gunnard was getting ready to grab Nancy by the tail. Lonnie sat up, twisting his neck until he caught a glimpse of Clem Henry at the other corner of the filling station. Clem was staring at him with unmistakable meaning, with the same look in his eyes he had had that afternoon when he said that nobody who worked for Arch Gunnard ought to stand for short-rationing. Lonnie lowered his eyes. He could not figure out how a Negro could be braver than he was. There were a lot of times like that when he would have given anything he had to be able to jump into Clem's shoes and change places with him.

"The trouble with this hound of yours, Lonnie, is that he's too heavy on his feet. Don't you reckon it would be a pretty slick little trick to lighten the load some, being as how he's a ketch hound to begin with?"

Lonnie remembered then what Clem Henry had said he would do if Arch Gunnard ever tried to cut off his dog's tail. Lonnie knew, and Clem knew, and everybody else knew, that that could give Arch the chance he was waiting for. All Arch asked, he had said, was for Clem Henry to overstep his place just one little half inch, or to talk back to him with just one little short word, and he would do the rest. Everybody knew what Arch meant by that, especially if Clem did not turn and run. And Clem had not been known to run from anybody, after fifteen years in the country.

Arch reached down and grabbed Nancy's tail while Lonnie was wondering about Clem. Nancy acted as if she thought Arch were playing some kind of a game with her. She turned her head around until she could reach Arch's hand to lick it. He cracked her on the bridge of the nose with the end of the jackknife.

"He's a mighty playful dog, Lonnie," Arch said, catching up a shorter grip on the tail, "but his wagpole is way too long for a dog his size, especially when he wants to be a ketch hound."

Lonnie swallowed hard.

"Mr. Arch, she's a mighty fine rabbit tracker. I —"

"Shucks, Lonnie," Arch said, whetting the knife blade on the dog's tail, "I ain't ever seen a hound in all my life that needed a tail that long to hunt rabbits with. It's way too long for just a common, ordinary, everyday ketch hound."

Lonnie looked up hopefully at Dudley Smith and the others. None of them offered any help. It was useless for him to try to stop Arch, because Arch Gunnard would let nothing stand in his way when once he had set his head on what he wished to do. Lonnie knew that if he should let himself show any anger or resentment, Arch would drive him off the farm before sundown that night. Clem Henry was the only person there who would help him, but Clem . . .

The white men and the Negroes at both corners of the filling station waited to see what Lonnie was going to do about it. All of them hoped he would put up a fight for his hound. If anyone ever had the nerve to stop Arch Gunnard from cutting off a dog's tail, it might put an end to it. It was plain, though, that Lonnie, who was one of Arch's sharecroppers, was afraid to speak up. Clem Henry might; Clem was the only one who might try to stop Arch, even if it meant trouble. And all of them knew that Arch would insist on running Clem out of the country, or filling him full of lead.

"I reckon it's all right with you, ain't it, Lonnie?" Arch said. "I don't seem to hear no objections."

Clem Henry stepped forward several paces, and stopped.

Arch laughed, watching Lonnie's face, and jerked Nancy to her feet. The hound cried out in pain and surprise, but Arch made her be quiet by kicking her in the belly.

Lonnie winced. He could hardly bear to see anybody kick his dog like that.

"Mr. Arch, I . . ."

A contraction in his throat almost choked him for several moments, and he had to open his mouth wide and fight for breath. The other white men around him were silent. Nobody liked to see a dog kicked in the belly like that.

Lonnie could see the other end of the filling station from the corner of his eye. He saw a couple of Negroes go up behind Clem and grasp his overalls. Clem spat on the ground, between outspread feet, but he did not try to break away from them.

"Being as how I don't hear no objections, I reckon it's all right to go ahead and cut it off," Arch said, spitting.

Lonnie's head went forward and all he could see of Nancy was her hind feet. He had come to ask for a slab of sowbelly and some molasses, or something. Now he did not know if he could ever bring himself to ask for rations, no matter how much hungrier they became at home.

"I always make it a habit of asking a man first," Arch said. "I wouldn't want to go ahead and cut off a tail if a man had any objections. That wouldn't be right. No, sir, it just wouldn't be fair and square."

Arch caught a shorter grip on the hound's tail and placed the knife blade on it two or three inches from the rump. It looked to those who were watching as if his mouth were watering, because tobacco juice began to trickle down the corners of his lips. He brought up the back of his hand and wiped his mouth.

A noisy automobile came plowing down the road through the deep red dust. Everyone looked up as it passed in order to see who was in it.

Lonnie glanced at it, but he could not keep his eyes raised. His head fell downward once more until he could feel his sharp chin cutting into his chest. He wondered then if Arch had noticed how lean his face was.

"I keep two or three ketch hounds around my place," Arch said, honing the blade on the tail of the dog as if it were a razor strop until his actions brought smiles to the faces of the men grouped around him, "but I never could see the sense of a ketch hound having a long tail. It only gets in their way when I send them out to catch a pig or a rabbit for my supper."

Pulling with his left hand and pushing with his right, Arch Gunnard docked the hound's tail as quickly and as easily as if he were cutting a willow switch in the pasture to drive the cows home with. The dog sprang forward with the release of her tail until she was far beyond Arch's reach, and began howling so loud she could be heard half a mile away. Nancy stopped once and looked back at Arch, and then she sprang to the middle of the road and began leaping and twisting in circles. All that time she was yelping and biting at the bleeding stub of her tail.

Arch leaned backward and twirled the severed tail in one hand while he wiped his jackknife blade on his boot sole. He watched Lonnie's dog chasing herself around in circles in the red dust.

Nobody had anything to say then. Lonnie tried not to watch his dog's agony, and he forced himself to keep from looking at Clem Henry. Then, with his eyes shut, he wondered why he had remained on Arch Gunnard's plantation all those past years, sharecropping for a mere living on short rations, and becoming leaner and leaner all the time. He knew then how true it was what Clem had said about Arch's sharecroppers' faces becoming sharp enough to hew their own coffins. His hand dropped when he had felt the bones of jaw and the exposed tendons of his cheeks.

As hungry as he was, he knew that even if Arch did give him some rations then, there would not be nearly enough for them to eat for the following week. Hatty, his wife, was already broken down from hunger and work in the fields, and his father, Mark Newsome, stone-deaf for the past twenty years, was always asking him why there was never enough food in the house for them to have a solid meal. Lonnie's head fell forward a little more, and he could feel his eyes becoming damp.

The pressure of his sharp chin against his chest made him so uncomfortable that he had to raise his head at last in order to ease the pain of it.

The first thing he saw when he looked up was Arch Gunnard twirling Nancy's tail in his left hand. Arch Gunnard had a trunk full of dogs' tails at home. He had been cutting off tails ever since anyone could remember, and during all those years he had accumulated a collection of which he was so proud that he kept the trunk locked and the key tied around his neck on a string. On Sunday afternoons when the preacher came to visit, or when a crowd was there to loll on the front porch and swap stories, Arch showed them off, naming each tail from memory just as well as if he had had a tag on it.

Clem Henry had left the filling station and was walking alone down the road towards the plantation. Clem Henry's house was in a cluster of Negro cabins below Arch's big house, and he had to pass Lonnie's house to get there. Lonnie was on the verge of getting up and leaving when he saw Arch looking at him. He did not know whether Arch was looking at his lean face, or whether he was watching to see if he were going to get up and go down the road with Clem.

The thought of leaving reminded him of his reason for being there. He had to have some rations before suppertime that night, no matter how short they were.

"Mr. Arch, I . . ."

Arch stared at him for a moment, appearing as if he had turned to listen to some strange sound unheard of before that moment.

Lonnie bit his lips, wondering if Arch was going to say anything about how lean and hungry he looked. But Arch was thinking about something else. He slapped his hand on his leg and laughed out loud.

"I sometimes wish niggers had tails," Arch said, coiling Nancy's tail into a ball and putting into his pocket. "I'd a heap rather cut off nigger tails than dog tails. There'd be more to cut, for one thing."

Dudley Smith and somebody else behind them laughed for a brief moment. The laughter died out almost as suddenly as it had risen.

The Negroes who had heard Arch shuffled their feet in the dust and moved backwards. It was only a few minutes until not one was left at the filling station. They went up the road behind the red wooden building until they were out of sight.

Arch got up and stretched. The sun was getting low, and it was no longer comfortable in the October air. "Well, I reckon I'll be getting on home to get me some supper," he said.

He walked slowly to the middle of the road and stopped to look at Nancy retreating along the ditch.

"Nobody going my way?" he asked. "What's wrong with you, Lonnie? Going home to supper, ain't you?"

"Mr. Arch, I . . ."

Lonnie found himself jumping to his feet. His first thought was to ask for the sowbelly and molasses, and maybe some corn meal; but when he opened his mouth, the words refused to come out. He took several steps forward and shook his head. He did not know what Arch might say or do if he said "No."

"Hatty'll be looking for you," Arch said, turning his back and walking off.

He reached into his hip pocket and took out Nancy's tail. He began twirling it as he walked down the road towards the big house in the distance.

Dudley Smith went inside the filling station, and the others walked away.

After Arch had gone several hundred yards, Lonnie sat down heavily on the box beside the gas pump from which he had got up when Arch spoke to him. He sat down heavily, his shoulders drooping, his arms falling between his outspread legs.

Lonnie did not know how long his eyes had been closed, but when he opened them, he saw Nancy lying between his feet, licking the docked tail. While he watched her, he felt the sharp point of his chin cutting into his chest again. Presently the door behind him was slammed shut, and a minute later he could hear Dudley Smith walking away from the filling station on his way home.

II

Lonnie had been sleeping fitfully for several hours when he suddenly found himself wide awake. Hatty shook him again. He raised himself on his elbow and tried to see into the darkness of the room. Without knowing what time it was, he was able to determine that it was still nearly two hours until sunrise.

"Lonnie," Hatty said again, trembling in the cold night air, "Lonnie, your pa ain't in the house."

Lonnie sat upright in bed.

"How do you know he ain't?" he said.

"I've been lying here wide awake ever since I got in bed, and I heard him when he went out. He's been gone all that time."

"Maybe he just stepped out for a while," Lonnie said, turning and trying to see through the bedroom window.

"I know what I'm saying, Lonnie," Hatty insisted. "Your pa's been gone a heap too long."

Both of them sat without a sound for several minutes while they listened for Mark Newsome.

Lonnie got up and lit a lamp. He shivered while he was putting on his shirt, overalls, and shoes. He tied his shoelaces in hard knots because he couldn't see in the faint light. Outside the window it was almost pitch-dark, and Lonnie could feel the damp October air blowing against his face.

"I'll go help look," Hatty said, throwing the covers off and starting to get up.

Lonnie went to the bed and drew the covers back over her and pushed her back into place.

"You try to get some sleep, Hatty," he said; "you can't stay awake the whole night. I'll go bring Pa back."

He left Hatty, blowing out the lamp, and stumbled through the dark hall, feeling his way to the front porch by touching the wall with his hands. When he got to the porch, he could still barely see any distance ahead, but his eyes were becoming more accustomed to the darkness. He waited a minute, listening.

Feeling his way down the steps into the yard, he walked around the corner of the house and stopped to listen again before calling his father.

"Oh, Pa!" he said loudly. "Oh, Pa!"

He stopped under the bedroom window when he realized what he had been doing.

"Now that's a fool thing for me to be out here doing," he said, scolding himself. "Pa couldn't hear it thunder."

He heard a rustling of the bed.

"He's been gone long enough to get clear to the crossroads, or more," Hatty said, calling through the window.

"Now you lay down and try to get a little sleep, Hatty," Lonnie told her. "I'll bring him back in no time."

He could hear Nancy scratching fleas under the house, but he knew she was in no condition to help look for Mark. It would be several days before she recovered from the shock of losing her tail.

"He's been gone a long time," Hatty said, unable to keep still.

"That don't make no difference," Lonnie said. "I'll find him sooner or later. Now you go on to sleep like I told you, Hatty."

Lonnie walked towards the barn, listening for some sound. Over at the big house he could hear the hogs grunting and squealing, and he wished they would be quiet so he could hear other sounds. Arch Gunnard's dogs were howling occasionally, but they were not making any more noise than they usually did at night, and he was accustomed to their howling.

Lonnie went to the barn, looking inside and out. After walking around the barn, he went into the field as far as the cotton shed. He knew it was useless, but he could not keep from calling his father time after time.

"Oh, Pa!" he said, trying to penetrate the darkness.

He went farther into the field.

"Now, what in the world could have become of Pa?" he said, stopping and wondering where to look next.

After he had gone back to the front yard, he began to feel uneasy for the first time. Mark had not acted any more strangely during the past week than he ordinarily did, but Lonnie knew he was upset over the way Arch Gunnard was giving out short rations. Mark had even said that, at the rate they were being fed, all of them would starve to death inside another three months.

Lonnie left the yard and went down the road towards the Negro cabins. When he got to Clem's house, he turned in and walked up the path to the door. He knocked several times and waited. There was no answer, and he rapped louder.

"Who's that?" he heard Clem say from bed.

"It's me," Lonnie said. "I've got to see you a minute, Clem. I'm out in the front yard."

He sat down and waited for Clem to dress and come outside. While he waited, he strained his ears to catch any sound that might be in the air. Over the fields towards the big house he could hear the fattening hogs grunt and squeal.

Clem came out and shut the door. He stood on the doorsill a moment speaking to his wife in bed, telling her he would be back and not to worry.

"Who's that?" Clem said, coming down into the yard.

Lonnie got up and met Clem halfway.

"What's the trouble?" Clem asked then, buttoning up his overall jumper.

"Pa's not in his bed," Lonnie said, "and Hatty says he's been gone from the house most all night. I went out in the field, and all around the barn, but I couldn't find a trace of him anywhere."

Clem then finished buttoning his jumper and began rolling a cigarette. He walked slowly down the path to the road. It was still dark, and it would be at least an hour before dawn made it any lighter.

"Maybe he was too hungry to stay in bed any longer," Clem said. "When I saw him yesterday, he said he was so shrunk up and weak he didn't know if he could last much longer. He looked like his skin and bones couldn't shrivel much more."

"I asked Arch last night after suppertime for some rations — just a little piece of sowbelly and some molasses. He said he'd get around to letting me have some the first thing this morning."

"Why don't you tell him to give you full rations or none?" Clem said. "If you knew you wasn't going to get none at all, you could move away and find a better man to sharecrop for, couldn't you?"

"I've been loyal to Arch Gunnard for a long time now," Lonnie said. "I'd hate to haul off and leave him like that."

Clem looked at Lonnie, but he did not say anything more just then. They turned up the road towards the driveway that led up to the big house. The fattening hogs were still grunting and squealing in the pen, and one of Arch's hounds came down a cotton row beside the driveway to smell their shoes.

"Them fattening hogs always get enough to eat," Clem said. "There's not a one of them that don't weigh seven hundred pounds right now, and they're getting bigger every day. Besides taking all that's thrown to them, they make a lot of meals off the chickens that get in there to peck around."

Lonnie listened to the grunting of the hogs as they walked up the driveway towards the big house.

"Reckon we'd better get Arch up to help look for Pa?" Lonnie said. "I'd hate to wake him up, but I'm scared Pa might stray off into the swamp and get lost for good. He couldn't hear it thunder, even. I never could find him back there in all that tangle if he got into it."

Clem said something under his breath and went on towards the barn and hog pen. He reached the pen before Lonnie got there.

"You'd better come here quick," Clem said, turning around to see where Lonnie was.

Lonnie ran to the hog pen. He stopped and climbed halfway up the wooden-and-wire sides of the fence. At first he could see nothing, but gradually he was able to see the moving mass of black fattening hogs on the other side of the pen. They were biting and snarling at each other like a pack of hungry hounds turned loose on a dead rabbit.

Lonnie scrambled to the top of the fence, but Clem caught him and pulled him back.

"Don't go in that hog pen that way," he said. "Them hogs will tear you to pieces, they're that wild. They're fighting over something."

Both of them ran around the corner of the pen and got to the side where the hogs were. Down under their feet on the ground Lonnie caught a glimpse of a dark mass splotched with white. He was able to see it for a moment only, because one of the hogs trampled over it.

Clem opened and closed his mouth several times before he was able to say anything at all. He clutched at Lonnie's arm, shaking him.

"That looks like it might be your pa," he said. "I swear before goodness, Lonnie, it does look like it."

Lonnie still could not believe it. He climbed to the top of the fence and began kicking his feet at the hogs, trying to drive them away. They paid no attention to him.

While Lonnie was perched there, Clem had gone to the wagon shed, and he ran back with two singletrees he had somehow managed to find there in the dark. He handed one to Lonnie, poking it at him until Lonnie's attention was drawn from the hogs long enough to take it.

Clem leaped over the fence and began swinging the singletree at the hogs. Lonnie slid down beside him, yelling at them. One hog turned on Lonnie and snapped at him, and Clem struck it over the back of the neck with enough force to drive it off momentarily.

By then Lonnie was able to realize what had happened. He ran to the mass of hogs, kicking them with his heavy stiff shoes and striking them on their heads with the iron-tipped singletree. Once he felt a stinging sensation, and looked down to see one of the hogs biting the calf of his leg. He had just enough time to hit the hog and drive it away before his leg was torn. He knew most of his overall leg had been ripped away, because he could feel the night air on his bare wet calf. .

Clem had gone ahead and had driven the hogs back. There was no other way to do anything. They were in a snarling circle around them, and both of them had to keep the singletrees swinging back and forth all the time to keep the hogs off. Finally Lonnie reached down and got a grip on Mark's leg. With Clem helping, Lonnie carried his father to the fence and lifted him over to the other side.

They were too much out of breath for a while to say anything, or to do anything else. The snarling, fattening hogs were at the fence, biting the wood and wire, and making more noise than ever.

While Lonnie was searching in his pockets for a match, Clem struck one. He held the flame close to Mark Newsome's head.

They both stared unbelievingly, and then Clem blew out the match. There was nothing said as they stared at each other in the darkness.

Clem walked several steps away, and turned and came back beside Lonnie.

"It's him, though," Clem said, sitting down on the ground. "It's him, all right."

"I reckon so," Lonnie said. He could think of nothing else to say then.

They sat on the ground, one on each side of Mark, looking at the body. There had been no sign of life in the body beside them since they had first touched it. The face, throat, and stomach had been completely devoured.

"You'd better go wake up Arch Gunnard," Clem said after a while.

"What for?" Lonnie said. "He can't help none now. It's too late for help."

"Makes no difference," Clem insisted. "You'd better go wake him up and let him see what there is to see. If you wait till morning, he might take it into his head to say the hogs didn't do it. Right now is the time to get him up so he can see what his hogs did."

Clem turned around and looked at the big house. The dark outline against the dark sky made him hesitate.

"A man who short-rations tenants ought to have to sit and look at that till it's buried."

Lonnie looked at Clem fearfully. He knew Clem was right, but he was scared to hear a Negro say anything like that about a white man.

"You oughtn't talk like that about Arch," Lonnie said. "He's in bed asleep. He didn't have a thing to do with it. He didn't have no more to do with it than I did."

Clem laughed a little, and threw the singletree on the ground between his feet. After letting it lie there a little while, he picked it up and began beating the ground with it.

Lonnie got to his feet slowly. He had never seen Clem act like that before, and he did not know what to think about it. He left without saying anything and walked stiffly to the house in the darkness to wake up Arch Gunnard.

III

Arch was hard to wake up. And even after he was awake, he was in no hurry to get up. Lonnie was standing outside the bedroom window, and Arch was lying in bed six or eight feet away. Lonnie could hear him toss and grumble.

"Who told you to come and wake me up in the middle of the night?" Arch said.

"Well, Clem Henry's out here, and he said maybe you'd like to know about it."

Arch tossed around on the bed, flailing the pillow with his fists.

"You tell Clem Henry I said that one of these days he's going to find himself turned inside out, like a coat sleeve."

Lonnie waited doggedly. He knew Clem was right in insisting that Arch ought to wake up and come out there to see what had happened. Lonnie was afraid to go back to the barnyard and tell Clem that Arch was not coming. He did not know, but he had a feeling that Clem might go into the bedroom and drag Arch out of bed. He did not like to think of anything like that taking place.

"Are you still out there, Lonnie?" Arch shouted.

"I'm right here, Mr. Arch. I —"

"If I wasn't so sleepy, I'd come out there and take a stick and — I don't know what I wouldn't do!"

Lonnie met Arch at the back step. On the way out to the hog pen Arch did not speak to him. Arch walked heavily ahead, not even waiting to see if Lonnie was coming. The lantern that Arch was carrying cast long flat beams of yellow light over the ground; and when they got to where Clem was waiting beside Mark's body, the Negro's face shone in the night like a highly polished plowshare.

"What was Mark doing in my hog pen at night, anyway?" Arch said, shouting at them both.

Neither Clem nor Lonnie replied. Arch glared at them for not answering. But no matter how many times he looked at them, his eyes returned each time to stare at the torn body of Mark Newsome on the ground at his feet.

"There's nothing to be done now," Arch said finally. "We'll just have to wait till daylight and send for the undertaker." He walked a few steps away. "Looks like you could have waited till morning in the first place. There wasn't no sense in getting me up."

He turned his back and looked sideways at Clem. Clem stood up and look him straight in the eyes.

"What do you want, Clem Henry?" he said. "Who told you to be coming around my house in the middle of the night? I don't want niggers coming here except when I send for them."

"I couldn't stand to see anybody eaten up by the hogs, and not do anything about it," Clem said.

"You mind your own business," Arch told him. "And when you talk to me, take off your hat, or you'll be sorry for it. It wouldn't take much to make me do you up the way you belong."

Lonnie backed away. There was a feeling of uneasiness around them. That was how trouble between Clem and Arch always began. He had seen it start that way dozens of times before. As long as Clem turned and went away, nothing happened, but sometimes he stayed right where he was and talked up to Arch just as if he had been a white man, too.

Lonnie hoped it would not happen this time. Arch was already mad enough about being waked up in the middle of the night, and Lonnie knew there was no limit to what Arch would do when he got good and mad at a Negro. Nobody had ever seen him kill a Negro, but he had said he had, and he told people that he was not scared to do it again.

"I reckon you know how he came to get eaten up by the hogs like that," Clem said, looking straight at Arch.

Arch whirled around.

"Are you talking to me . . .?"

"I asked you that," Clem stated.

"God damn you, yellow-blooded . . ." Arch yelled.

He swung the lantern at Clem's head. Clem dodged, but the bottom of it hit his shoulder, and it was smashed to pieces. The oil splattered on the ground, igniting in the air from the flaming wick. Clem was lucky not to have it splash on his face and overalls.

"Now, look here . . ." Clem said.

"You yellow-blooded nigger," Arch said, rushing at him. "I'll teach you to talk back to me. You've got too big for your place for the last time. I've been taking too much from you, but I ain't doing it no more."

"Mr. Arch, I . . ." Lonnie said, stepping forward partly between them. No one heard him.

Arch stood back and watched the kerosene flicker out on the ground.

"You know good and well why he got eaten up by the fattening hogs," Clem said, standing his ground. "He was so hungry he had to get up out of bed in the middle of the night and come up here in the dark trying to find something to eat. Maybe he was trying to find the smokehouse. It makes no difference, either way. He's been on short rations like everybody else working on your place, and he was so old he didn't know where else to look for food except in your smokehouse. You know good and well that's how he got lost up here in the dark and fell in the hog pen."

The kerosene had died out completely. In the last faint flare, Arch had reached down and grabbed up the singletree that had been lying on the ground where Lonnie had dropped it.

Arch raised the singletree over his head and struck with all his might at Clem. Clem dodged, but Arch drew back again quickly and landed a blow on his arm just above the elbow before Clem could dodge it. Clem's arm dropped to his side, dangling lifelessly.

"You God-damn yellow-blooded nigger!" Arch shouted. "Now's your time, you black bastard! I've been waiting for the chance to teach you your lesson. And this's going to be one you won't never forget."

Clem felt the ground with his feet until he had located the other singletree. He stooped down and got it. Raising it, he did not try to hit Arch, but held it in front of him so he could ward off Arch's blows at his head. He continued to stand his ground, not giving Arch an inch.

"Drop that singletree," Arch said.

"I won't stand here and let you beat me like that," Clem protested.

"By God, that's all I want to hear," Arch said, his mouth curling. "Nigger, your time has come, by God!"

He swung once more at Clem, but Clem turned and ran towards the barn. Arch went after him a few steps and stopped. He threw aside the singletree and turned and ran back to the house.

Lonnie went to the fence and tried to think what was best for him to do. He knew he could not take sides with a Negro, in the open, even if Clem had helped him, and especially after Clem had talked to Arch in the way he wished he could himself. He was a white man, and to save his life he could not stand to think of turning against Arch, no matter what happened.

Presently a light burst through one of the windows of the house, and he heard Arch shouting at his wife to wake her up.

When he saw Arch's wife go to the telephone, Lonnie realized what was going to happen. She was calling up the neighbors and Arch's friends. They would not mind getting up in the night when they found out what was going to take place.

Out behind the barn he could hear Clem calling him. Leaving the yard, Lonnie felt his way out there in the dark.

"What's the trouble, Clem?" he said.

"I reckon my time has come," Clem said. "Arch Gunnard talks that way when he's good and mad. He talked just like he did that time he carried Jim Moffin off to the swamp — and Jim never came back."

"Arch wouldn't do anything like that to you, Clem," Lonnie said excitedly, but he knew better.

Clem said nothing.

"Maybe you'd better strike out for the swamps till he changes his mind and cools off some," Lonnie said. "You might be right, Clem."

Lonnie could feel Clem's eyes burning into him.

"Wouldn't be no sense in that, if you'd help me," Clem said. "Wouldn't you stand by me?"

Lonnie trembled as the meaning of Clem's suggestion became clear to him. His back was to the side of the barn, and he leaned against it while sheets of black and white passed before his eyes.

"Wouldn't you stand by me?" Clem asked again.

"I don't know what Arch would say to that," Lonnie told him haltingly.

Clem walked away several paces. He stood with his back to Lonnie while he looked across the field towards the quarter where his home was.

"I could go in that little patch of woods out there and stay till they get tired of looking for me," Clem said, turning around to see Lonnie.

"You'd better go somewhere," Lonnie said uneasily. "I know Arch Gunnard. He's hard to handle when he makes up his mind to do something he wants to do. I couldn't stop him an inch. Maybe you'd better get clear out of the country, Clem."

"I couldn't do that, and leave my family down there across the field," Clem said.

"He's going to get you if you don't."

"If you'd only sort of help me out a little, he wouldn't. I would only have to go and hide out in that little patch of woods over there a while. Looks like you could do that for me, being as how I helped you find your pa when he was in the pig pen."

Lonnie nodded, listening for sounds from the big house. He continued to nod at Clem while Clem was waiting to be assured.

"If you're going to stand up for me," Clem said, "I can just go over there in the woods and wait till they get it off their minds. You won't be telling them where I'm at, and you could say I struck out for the swamp. They wouldn't ever find me without bloodhounds."

"That's right," Lonnie said, listening for sounds of Arch's coming out of the house. He did not wish to be found back there behind the barn where Arch could accuse him of talking to Clem.

The moment Lonnie replied, Clem turned and ran off into the night. Lonnie went after him a few steps, as if he had suddenly changed his mind about helping him, but Clem was lost in the darkness by then.

Lonnie waited for a few minutes, listening to Clem crashing through the underbrush in the patch of woods a quarter of a mile away. When he could hear Clem no longer, he went around the barn to meet Arch.

Arch came out of the house carrying his double-barreled shotgun and the lantern he had picked up in the house. His pockets were bulging with shells.

"Where is that damn nigger, Lonnie?" Arch asked him. "Where'd he go to?"

Lonnie opened his mouth, but no words came out.

"You know which way he went, don't you?"

Lonnie again tried to say something, but there were no sounds. He jumped when he found himself nodding his head to Arch.

"Mr. Arch, I —"

"That's all right, then," Arch said. "That's all I need to know now, Dudley Smith and Tom Hawkins and Frank and Dave Howard and the rest will be here in a minute, and you can stay right here so you can show us where he's hiding out."

Frantically Lonnie tried to say something. Then he reached for Arch's sleeve to stop him, but Arch had gone.

Arch ran around the house to the front yard. Soon a car came racing down the road, its headlights lighting up the whole place, hog pen and all. Lonnie knew it was probably Dudley Smith, because his was the first house in that direction, only half a mile away. While he was turning into the driveway, several other automobiles came into sight, both up the road and down it.

Lonnie trembled. He was afraid Arch was going to tell him to point out where Clem had gone to hide. Then he knew Arch would tell him. He had promised Clem he would not do that. But try as he might, he could not make himself believe that Arch Gunnard would do anything more than whip Clem.

Clem had not done anything that called for lynching. He had not raped a white woman, he had not shot at a white man; he had only talked back to Arch, with his hat on. But Arch was mad enough to do anything; he was mad enough at Clem not to stop at anything short of lynching.

The whole crowd of men was swarming around him before he realized it. And there was Arch clutching his arm and shouting into his face.

"Mr. Arch, I —"

Lonnie recognized every man in the feeble dawn. They were excited, and they looked like men on the last lap of an all-night fox-hunting party. Their shotguns and pistols were held at their waist, ready for the kill.

"What's the matter with you, Lonnie?" Arch said, shouting into his ear. "Wake up and say where Clem Henry went to hide out. We're ready to go get him."

Lonnie remembered looking up and seeing Frank Howard dropping yellow twelve-gauge shells into the breech of his gun. Frank bent forward so he could hear Lonnie tell Arch where Clem was hiding.

"You ain't going to kill Clem this time, are you, Mr. Arch?" Lonnie asked.

"Kill him?" Dudley Smith repeated. "What do you reckon I've been waiting all this time for if it wasn't for a chance to get Clem. That nigger has had it coming to him ever since he came to this county. He's a bad nigger, and it's coming to him."

"It wasn't exactly Clem's fault," Lonnie said. "If Pa hadn't come up here and fell in the hog pen, Clem wouldn't have had a thing to do with it. He was helping me, that's all."

"Shut up, Lonnie," somebody shouted at him. "You're so excited you don't know what you're saying. You're taking up for a nigger when you talk like that."

People were crowding around him so tightly he felt as if he were being squeezed to death. He had to get some air, get his breath, get out of the crowd.

"That's right," Lonnie said.

He heard himself speak, but he did not know what he was saying.

"But Clem helped me find Pa when he got lost looking around for something to eat."

"Shut up, Lonnie," somebody said again. "You damn fool, shut up!"

Arch grabbed his shoulder and shook him until his teeth rattled. Then Lonnie realized what he had been saying.

"Now, look here, Lonnie," Arch shouted. "You must be out of your head, because you know good and well you wouldn't talk like a niggerlover in your right mind."

"That's right," Lonnie said, trembling all over. "I sure wouldn't want to talk like that."

He could still feel the grip on his shoulder where Arch's strong fingers had hurt him.

"Did Clem go to the swamp, Lonnie?" Dudley Smith said. "Is that right, Lonnie?"

Lonnie tried to shake his head; he tried to nod his head. Then Arch's fingers squeezed his thin neck. Lonnie looked at the men wild-eyed.

"Where's Clem hiding, Lonnie?" Arch demanded, squeezing.

Lonnie went three or four steps towards the barn. When he stopped, the men behind him pushed forward again. He found himself being rushed behind the barn and beyond it.

"All right, Lonnie," Arch said. "Now which way?"

Lonnie pointed towards the patch of woods where the creek was. The swamp was in the other direction.

"He said he was going to hide out in that little patch of woods along the creek over there, Mr. Arch," Lonnie said. "I reckon he's over there now."

Lonnie felt himself being swept forward, and he stumbled over the rough ground trying to keep from being knocked down and trampled upon. Nobody was talking, and everyone seemed to be walking on tiptoes. The gray light of early dawn was increasing enough both to hide them and to show the way ahead.

Just before they reached the fringe of the woods, the men separated, and Lonnie found himself a part of the circle that was closing in on Clem.

Lonnie was alone, and there was nobody to stop him, but he was unable to move forward or backward. It began to be clear to him what he had done.

Clem was probably up a tree somewhere in the woods ahead, but by that time he had been surrounded on all sides. If he should attempt to break and run, he would be shot down like a rabbit.

Lonnie sat down on a log and tried to think what to do. The sun would be up in a few more minutes, and as soon as it came up, the men would close in on the creek and Clem. He would have no chance at all among all those shotguns and pistols.

Once or twice he saw the flare of a match through the underbrush where some of the men were lying in wait. A whiff of cigarette smoke struck his nostrils, and he found himself wondering if Clem could smell it wherever he was in the woods.

There was still no sound anywhere around him, and he knew that Arch Gunnard and the rest of the men were waiting for the sun, which would in a few minutes come up behind him in the east.

It was light enough by that time to see plainly the rough ground and the tangled underbrush and the curling bark on the pine trees.

The men had already begun to creep forward, guns raised as if stalking a deer. The woods were not large, and the circle of men would be able to cover it in a few minutes at the rate they were going forward. There was still a chance that Clem had slipped through the circle before dawn broke, but Lonnie felt that he was still there. He began to feel then that Clem was there because he himself had placed him there for the men to find more easily.

Lonnie found himself moving forward, drawn into the narrowing circle. Presently he could see the men all around him in dim outline. Their eyes were searching the heavy green pine tops as they went forward from tree to tree.

"Oh, Pa!" he said in a hoarse whisper. "Oh, Pa!"

He went forward a few steps, looking into the bushes and up into the treetops. When he saw the other men again, he realized that it was not Mark Newsome being sought. He did not know what had made him forget like that.

The creeping forward began to work into the movement of Lonnie's body. He found himself springing forward on his toes, and his body was leaning in that direction. It was like creeping up on a rabbit when you did not have a gun to hunt with.

He forgot again what he was doing there. The springing motion in his legs seemed to be growing stronger with each step. He bent forward so far he could almost touch the ground with his fingertips. He could not stop now. He was keeping up with the circle of men.

The fifteen men were drawing closer and closer together. The dawn had broken enough to show the time on the face of a watch. The sun was beginning to color the sky above.

Lonnie was far in advance of anyone else by then. He could not hold himself back. The strength in his legs was more than he could hold in check.

He had for so long been unable to buy shells for his gun that he had forgotten how much he liked to hunt.

The sound of the men's steady creeping had become a rhythm in his ears.

"Here's the bastard!" somebody shouted, and there was a concerted crashing through the dry underbrush. Lonnie dashed forward, reaching the tree almost as quickly as anyone else.

He could see everybody with guns raised, and far into the sky above the sharply outlined face of Clem Henry gleamed in the rising sun. His body was hugging the slender top of the pine.

Lonnie did not know who was the first to fire, but the rest of the men did not hesitate. There was a deafening roar as the shotguns and revolvers flared and smoked around the trunk of the tree.

He closed his eyes; he was afraid to look again at the face above. The firing continued without break. Clem hugged the tree with all his might, and then, with the faraway sound of splintering wood, the top of the tree and Clem came crashing through the lower limbs to the ground. The body, sprawling and torn, landed on the ground with a thud that stopped Lonnie's heart for a moment.

He turned, clutching for the support of a tree, as the firing began once more. The crumpled body was tossed time after time, like a sackful of kittens being killed with an automatic shotgun, as charges of lead were fired into it from all sides. A cloud of dust rose from the ground and drifted overhead with the choking odor of burned powder.

Lonnie did not remember how long the shooting lasted. He found himself running from tree to tree, clutching at the rough pine bark, stumbling wildly towards the cleared ground. The sky had turned from gray to red when he emerged in the open, and as he ran, falling over the hard clods in the plowed field, he tried to keep his eyes on the house ahead.

Once he fell and found it almost impossible to rise again to his feet. He strugged to his knees, facing the round red sun. The warmth gave him the strength to rise to his feet, and he muttered unintelligibly to himself. He tried to say things he had never thought to say before.

When he got home, Hatty was waiting for him in the yard. She had heard the shots in the woods, and she had seen him stumbling over the hard clods in the field, and she had seen him kneeling there looking straight into the face of the sun. Hatty was trembling as she ran to Lonnie to find out what the matter was.

Once in his own yard, Lonnie turned and looked for a second over his shoulder. He saw the men climbing over the fence at Arch Gunnard's. Arch's wife was standing on the back porch, and she was speaking to them.

"Where's your pa, Lonnie?" Hatty said. "And what in the world was all that shooting in the woods for?" Lonnie stumbled forward until he had reached the front porch. He fell upon the steps.

"Lonnie, Lonnie!" Hatty was saying. "Wake up and tell me what in the world is the matter. I've never seen the like of all that's going on."

"Nothing," Lonnie said. "Nothing."

"Well, if there's nothing the matter, can't you go up to the big house and ask for a little piece of streak-of-lean? We ain't got a thing to cook for breakfast. Your pa's going to be hungrier than ever after being up walking around all night."

"What?" Lonnie said, his voice rising to a shout as he jumped to his feet.

"Why, I only said go up to the big house and get a little piece of streak-of-lean, Lonnie. That's all I said."

He grabbed his wife about the shoulders.

"Meat?" he yelled, shaking her roughly.

"Yes," she said, pulling away from him in surprise. "Couldn't you go ask Arch Gunnard for a little bit of streak-of-lean?"

Lonnie slumped down again on the steps, his hands falling between his outspread legs and his chin falling on his chest.

"No," he said almost inaudibly. "No. I ain't hungry."

(First published in 1935 in *Scribner's*)

Ours Were
Idle Pleasures . . .

Blue Boy

Two hours after dinner they were still sitting in the airtight overheated parlor. A dull haze of tobacco smoke was packed in layers from the tabletop to the ceiling, and around the chairs hovered the smell of dried perspiration and stale perfume. The New Year's Day turkey-and-hog dinner had made the women droopy and dull-eyed; the men were stretched out in their chairs with their legs spread out and their heads thrown back, looking as if around each swollen belly a hundred feet of stuffed sausage-casing had been wound.

Grady Walters sat up, rubbed his red-veined face, and looked at his guests. After a while he went to the door and called for one of his Negro servants. He sent the Negro on the run for Blue Boy.

After he had closed the door tightly, Grady walked back towards his chair, looking at the drowsy men and women through the haze of blue tobacco smoke. It had been more than an hour since anyone had felt like saying anything.

"What time of day is it getting to be, Grady?" Rob Howard

asked, rubbing first his eyes and then his belly.

"Time to have a little fun," Grady said.

Blue Boy came through the back door and shuffled down the hall to the parlor where the people were. He dragged his feet sideways over the floor, making a sound like soybeans being poured into a wooden barrel.

"We been waiting here all afternoon for you to come in here and show the folks some fun, Blue Boy," Grady said. "All my visitors are just itching to laugh. Reckon you can make them shake their sides, Blue Boy?"

Blue Boy grinned at the roomful of men and women. He dug his hands into his overall pockets and made some kind of unintelligible sound in this throat.

Rob Howard asked Grady what Blue Boy could do. Several of the women sat up and began rubbing powder into the pores of their skin.

The colored boy grinned some more, stretching his neck in a semicircle.

"Blue Boy," Grady said, "show these white-folks how you caught that shoat the other day and bit him to death. Go on, Blue Boy! Let's see how you chewed that shoat to death with your teeth."

For several moments the boy's lips moved like eyelids a-flutter, and he made a dash for the door. Grady caught him by the shoulder and tossed him back into the center of the room.

"All right, Blue Boy," Grady shouted at him. "Do what I told you to do. Show the white-folks how you bit that pig to death."

Blue Boy made deeper sounds in his throat. What he said sounded more unintelligible than Gullah. Nobody but Grady could understand what he was trying to say.

"It don't make no difference if you ain't got a shoat here to kill," Grady answered him. "Go on and show the white-folks how you killed one the other day for me."

Blue Boy dropped on his hands and knees, making sounds as if he were trying to protest. Grady nudged him with his foot, prodding him on.

The Negro boy suddenly began to snarl and bite, acting as if he himself had been turned into a snarling, biting shoat. He grabbed into the air, throwing his arms around an imaginary young hog, and began to tear its throat with his sharp white teeth. The Howards and Hannafords crowded closer, trying to see the idiot go through the actions of a bloodthirsty maniac.

Down on the floor, Blue Boy's face was contorted and swollen. His eyes glistened, and his mouth drooled. He was doing all he could to please Grady Walters.

When he had finished, the Howards and Hannafords fell back, fanning their faces and wiping the backs of their hands with their handkerchiefs. Even Grady fanned his flushed face when Blue Boy stopped and rolled over on the floor exhausted.

"What else can he do, Grady?" the youngest of the Hannaford women asked.

"Anything I tell him to do," Grady said. "I've got Blue Boy trained. He does whatever I tell him."

They looked down at the small, thin, blue-skinned, seventeen-year-old Negro on the floor. His clothes were ragged, and his thick kinky hair was almost as long as a Negro woman's. He looked the same, except in size, as he did the day, twelve years before, when Grady brought him to the big house from one of the sharecroppers' cabins. Blue Boy had never become violent, and he obeyed every word of Grady's. Grady had taught him to do tricks as he would instruct a young puppy to roll over on his back when bidden. Blue Boy always obeyed, but sometimes he was not quick enough to suit Grady, and then Grady flew into him with the leather bellyband that hung on a nail on the back porch.

The Howards and Hannafords had sat down again, but the Negro boy still lay on the floor. Grady had not told him to get up.

"What's wrong with him, Grady?" Rob Howard asked.

"He ain't got a grain of sense," Grady said, laughing a little. "See how he grins all the time? A calf is born with more sense than he's got right now."

"Why don't you send him to the insane asylum, then?"

"What for?" Grady said. "He's more fun than a barrel of monkeys. I figure he's worth keeping just for the hell of it. If I sent him off to the asylum, I'd miss my good times with him. I wouldn't take a hundred dollars for Blue Boy."

"What else can he do?" Henry Hannaford asked.

"I'll show you," Grady said. "Here, Blue Boy, get up and do that monkeyshine dance for the white-folks. Show them what you can do with your feet."

Blue Boy got up, pushing himself erect with hands and feet. He stood grinning for a while at the men and women in a circle around him.

"Go on, Blue Boy, shake your feet for the white-folks," Grady told him, pointing at Blue Boy's feet. "Do the monkeyshine, Blue Boy."

The boy began to shuffle his shoes on the floor, barely raising them off the surface. Grady started tapping his feet, moving them faster and faster all the time. Blue Boy watched him, and after a while his own feet began going faster. He kept it up until he was dancing so fast his breath began to give out. His eyes were swelling, and it looked as if his balls would pop out of his head any moment. The arteries in his neck got larger and rounder.

"That nigger can do the monkeyshine better than any nigger I ever saw," Henry Hannaford said.

Blue Boy sank into a heap on the floor, the arteries in his neck pumping and swelling until some of the women in the room covered their faces to keep from seeing them.

It did not take Blue Boy long to get his wind back, but he still lay on the floor. Grady watched him until he thought he had recovered enough to stand up again.

"What else can your trained nigger do, Grady?" Rob Howard asked. "Looks like you would have learned him a heap of tricks in ten or twelve years' time."

"If it wasn't getting so late in the day, I'd tell him to do all he knows," Grady said. "I'll let him do one more, anyway."

Blue Boy had not moved from the floor.

"Get up, Blue Boy," Grady said. "Get up and stand up on your feet."

Blue Boy got up grinning. His head turned once more on his rubbery neck, stretching in a semicircle around the room. He grinned at the white faces about him.

"Take out that blacksnake and whip it to a frazzle," Grady told him. "Take it out, Blue Boy, and show the white-folks what you can do."

Blue Boy grinned, stretching his rubbery neck until it looked as if it would come loose from his body.

"What's he going to do now, Grady?" Rob Howard asked.

"You just wait and see, Rob," Grady said. "All right, Blue Boy, do like I said. Whip that blacksnake."

The youngest Hannaford woman giggled. Blue Boy turned and stared at her with his round white eyeballs. He grinned until Grady prodded him on.

"Now I reckon you folks know why I didn't send him off to the insane asylum," Grady said. "I have a heap more fun out of Blue Boy than I would with anything else you can think of. He can't hoe cotton, or pick it, and he hasn't even got enough sense to chop a piece of stovewood, but he makes up for all that by learning to do the tricks I teach him."

Once more Blue Boy's eyes began to pop in the sockets of his skull, and the arteries in his neck began to pump and swell. He dropped to his knees and his once rubbery neck was as rigid as a table leg. The grinning lines on his face had congealed into weltlike scars.

The Howards and Hannafords, who had come from five counties to eat Grady's New Year's Day turkey-and-hog dinner, gulped and wheezed at the sight of Blue Boy. He was beginning to droop like a wilting stalk of pigweed. Then he fell from his knees.

With his face pressed against the splintery floor, the grooves in his cheeks began to soften, and his grinning features glistened in the drying perspiration. His breathing became inaudible, and the swollen arteries in his neck were as rigid as taut-drawn ropes.

(First published in 1935 in *Anvil*)

Return to Lavinia

At first she did not know what had awakened her. She was not certain whether it had been a noise somewhere about the house, or whether it was the metallike burning of her feverish skin. By the time her eyes were fully open she could hear a bedlam of crowing, the sounds coming from every direction. For an hour at midnight the roosters crowed continually; from the chicken yards in town and from the farms surrounding the town, the sounds filled the flat country with an almost unbearable din.

Lavinia sat up in bed, wide awake after three hours of fitful sleep. She pressed the palms of her hands against her ears to shut out the crowing, but even that did not help any. She could still hear the sound no matter what she did to stop it.

"I'll never be able to go to sleep again," she said, holding her hands tight to the sides of her head. "I might as well stop trying."

When she looked up, there was a light shining through the rear windows and doors. The illumination spread over the back porch and cast a pale moonlike glow over the walls of her room. She sat tensely awake, holding her breath while she listened.

Presently the screen door at the end of the hall opened, squeaked shrilly, and slammed shut. She shivered while the small electric fan on the edge of her dresser whirred with a monotonous drone. In her excitement she clutched her shoulders in her arms, still shivering while the fan blew a steady stream of sultry air against her face and neck.

The footsteps became inaudible for a moment, then distinct. She would know them no matter where she heard them. For three years she had heard them, night and day since she was fifteen. Some footsteps changed from year to year; strides increased, strides decreased; leather-and-nail heels were changed to rubber, heel-and-toe treads became flat-footed shufflings; most footsteps changed, but his had remained the same during all that time.

Phil Glenn crossed the porch to the kitchen, the room next to hers, and snapped on the light. She shivered convulsively in the fan draft, gasping for breath in the sultry air.

Through the wall she could hear him open the icebox, chip off several chunks of ice, and drop them into a tumbler. When he dropped the lid of the icebox and crossed to the spigot, she could hear the flow of water until the tumbler filled and overflowed. Everything he did, every motion he made, was taking place before her eyes as plainly as if she were standing beside him while he chipped the ice and filled the tumbler to overflowing.

When he had finished, he turned off the light and went back out on the porch. He stood there, his handkerchief in hand, wiping his face and lips spasmodically while he listened as intently as she was listening.

There was a sound of someone else's walking in the front of the house. It was an unfamiliar sound, a sound that both of them heard and listened to for the first time.

When she could bear it no longer, Lavinia threw herself back upon the bed, covering her face with the pillow. No matter how hard she tried, she could not keep from sobbing into the pillow. As regularly as midnight came, she had cried like that every night since he had been away.

The next thing she knew, he was sitting on the edge of her bed trying to say something to her. She could not understand a word he was saying. Even after she had sat up again, she still did not know what it was. Long after he had stopped speaking, she stared at his features in the pale glow of reflected light. She tried to think of something either of them would have to say.

"We just got back," he said.

After he had spoken, she laughed at herself for not having known he would say exactly that.

"We went down to the beach for a few days when we left here," he finished.

Lavinia stared at him while she wondered what he expected her to say by way of comment or reply.

"I thought I told you where we were going, but after I left I remembered I hadn't. If we hadn't been halfway there, I'd have turned around and come back to tell you. I wouldn't want you to think—"

She laughed.

"—I wouldn't want you to think—" he said over again.

Lavinia threw her head back and laughed out loud. Her voice sounded soft and deep.

"Well, anyway," he said, "it was a mighty short honeymoon. But it was nice on the beach."

She laughed again, but the sound of her laughter was all but drowned out in the drone of the electric fan.

"It was just what you would expect," he said casually.

The electric fan was blowing her gown against her back with rippling motions. She moved sidewise to the fan so that nothing would prevent her from hearing every word he said. After she had settled down, he crossed his legs.

"I guess it's going to be all right," he said, looking through the window and back again at her. "It'll be all right."

Before he had finished, both of them turned to listen to the sound of footsteps in the front of the house. The sound echoed through the night.

In the closeness of the room, Lavinia could feel his heavy breathing vibrate the air. She wanted to say something to him, but she was afraid. She did not know what she could say. If she said the wrong thing, it would be a lot worse than not saying anything. She held her breath in perplexity.

He got up, went to the window, looked out into the darkness for a moment, and came back to stand beside her. She could feel him looking down at her even though she could not see him distinctly in the shadow he made when his back was to the door. She had to restrain herself from reaching out to feel if he were there beside her.

"Hannah is quite a girl," he said finally, laughing a little to hide his uneasiness.

She knew he would have to say something like that sooner or later. It was the only way to get it over with. After that she waited for him to go on.

"We'll get along all right," he said. "There won't be any trouble."

She shook her hair in the draft of the fan. All at once the fan seemed as if it were going faster than ever. The draft became stronger, the whirring sound rose in volume to an ear-splitting pitch, and her shoulders shook involuntarily in the fan's chill breeze.

"I thought I would have a hard time of it," he said, "but now that it's over, it wasn't half as bad as I thought it was going to be. We'll get along all right."

Lavinia reached out and found his hand in the dark. He sat down on the side of the bed while she tried to think what to say.

"What's the matter, Lavinia?" he asked her. "What's wrong?"

"Let me go, Phil," she begged, beginning to cry in her soft deep voice. "I want to go."

He shook his head unmistakably.

"I couldn't let you go now, Lavinia," he said earnestly. "We agreed about that before this business took place the other day. You promised me. If I hadn't believed you would keep your promise, I wouldn't have gone ahead and done it."

"Please, Phil," she begged, crying brokenly until her soft deep voice filled the room. "Please let me go."

He kept on shaking his head, refusing to listen to her. Suddenly, there rose once more the bedlam of crowing that lasted for an hour in intermittent bursts every midnight. Neither of them tried to say anything while the crowing was at its height.

After several minutes the drone of the fan and the sobs in her breast drowned out the roosters' crowing.

"I've got to go, Phil," she said, holding back her sobs while she spoke.

"I can't let you go," he said. "I just can't let you go, Lavinia."

She stopped crying and sat up more erectly, almost on her knees. He gazed at her wonderingly.

"I'm a nigger, Phil," she said slowly. "I'm a nigger — a cooking, cleaning, washing nigger."

"Shut up, Lavinia!" he said, shaking her until she was in pain. "Shut up, do you hear?"

"I am, and you know I am," she cried. "I'm a nigger — a cooking, cleaning, washing nigger — just like all the rest are."

She brushed the tears from her eyes and tried to look at him clearly in the half-light. She could see his deep, serious expression and she knew he meant every word he had said.

"You'll get over it in a few days," he told her. "Just wait awhile and see if everything doesn't turn out just like I say it will."

"You know what I am, though," she said uncontrollably.

"Shut up, Lavinia!" he said, shaking her some more. "You're not! You're a white girl with colored blood — and little of that. Any of us might be like that. I have colored blood in me, for all I know. Even *she* might have some."

He jerked his head toward the front of the house. Forgetting everything else momentarily, they both listened for a while. There was no sound whatever coming from that part of the building.

"She'll order me around just like she would anybody else," Lavinia said. "She'll treat me like the blackest washwoman you ever saw. She'll be as mean to me as she knows how, just to keep me in my place. She'll even call me 'nigger' sometimes."

"You're just excited now," he said. "It won't be like that tomorrow. You know as well as I do that I don't care what you are. Even if you looked like a colored girl, I wouldn't care. But you don't look like one — you look like a golden girl. That's all there is to it. If she ever says anything different, just don't pay any attention to her."

"She'll keep me in my place," Lavinia said. "I don't mind staying in my place, but I can't live here and have her tell me about it a dozen times a day. I want to go. I am going."

Phil got up, went to the door, and closed it. He came back and stood beside her.

"You're going to stay here, Lavinia," he said firmly. "If anybody goes, she'll have to go. I mean that."

Lavinia lay back on the pillow, closing her eyes and breathing deeply. She would rather have heard him say that than anything else he had said that night. She had been waiting five days and nights to hear him say it, and at last she could relax with the relief he had given her.

"I got married for a pretty good reason," he told her, "but I'm not going to let it ruin everything. I thought you understood all about it before it happened. You even told me to go ahead and marry her, so it would put a stop to all the talk about her living here as my housekeeper. It was hurting business at the store. We had to do something like that. And now you say you are going to leave."

There was silence for a long time after he had finished. Only the drone of the electric fan could be heard, and that for the first time sounded subdued.

"I won't leave," Lavinia said slowly, her voice so low he had to lean closer to her in order to hear. "The only way to make me leave is to throw me out. And I'd come back even if you did that. I want to stay, Phil."

As she lay on her back, she felt herself dropping into unconsciousness. For a while she made no effort to keep herself awake. She lay with her eyes closed and a smile on her lips.

She knew nothing else until he got up from the side of the bed. She opened her eyes as wide as she could in order to see if he was still there.

"I've got to go now," he said.

She sat up, shaking her head from side to side in the breeze of the electic fan. The air that blew through her hair was warm and clinging, and it began making her drowsy once more.

"Phil," she asked, "will you tell me something before you go?"

"Sure," he said, laughing. "What?"

"Phil, did you have a good time on your honeymoon?"

He laughed at her for a moment. After he had stopped there was a pause, and he laughed again.

"I had a great time on the beach," he said hesitatingly.

She laughed at him then, with motions of her head, in her soft deep voice.

"And with that old-maid schoolteacher you married, too?" she said, her words trailing off into soft deep laughter that filled the room.

He did not answer her. He went to the door to open it, but for several moments he did not turn the knob. He turned back to look at her again, her laughter filling his ears.

After a while he jerked open the door, stepped out on the porch, and closed the door as quickly as he could. He waited there for a moment to find out if Hannah had heard the laughter in Lavinia's room. When she did not come out into the hall after that length of time, he walked quickly down the porch to the hall door.

Lavinia's laughter swam through the hot night air, pouring into his ears until he could not hear even the sound of his own footsteps. The soft deep notes followed him like a familiar sound that was so close to him he could not find its source.

(First published in 1935 in *Esquire*)

August Afternoon

Vic Glover awoke with the noonday heat ringing in his ears. He had been asleep for only half an hour, and he was getting ready to turn over and go back to sleep when he opened his eyes for a moment and saw Hubert's woolly black head over the top of his bare toes. He stretched his eyelids and held them open in the glaring light as long as he could.

Hubert was standing in the yard, at the edge of the porch, with a pine cone in his hand.

Vic cursed him.

The colored man once more raked the cone over Vic's bare toes, tickling them on the underside, and stepped back out of reach.

"What do you mean by standing there tickling me with that dad-burned cone?" Vic shouted at Hubert. "Is that all you can find to do? Why don't you get out in the field and do something to them boll weevils? They're going to eat up every boll of cotton on the place if you don't stop them."

"I surely hated to wake you up, Mr. Vic," Hubert said, "but

there's a white man out here looking for something. He won't say what he's looking for, but he's hanging around waiting for it."

Vic sat up wide awake. He sat up on the quilt and pulled on his shoes without looking into the yard. The white sand in the yard beat the glare of the sun directly into his eyes and he could see nothing beyond the edge of the porch. Hubert threw the pine cone under the porch and stepped aside.

"He must be looking for trouble," Vic said. "When they come around and don't say anything, and just sit and look, it's trouble they're looking for."

"There he is, Mr. Vic," Hubert said, nodding his head across the yard. "There he sits up against that water-oak tree yonder."

Vic looked around for Willie. Willie was sitting on the top step at the other end of the porch, directly in front of the strange white man. She did not look at Vic.

"You ought to have better sense than to wake me up while I'm taking a nap. This is no time of the day to be up in the summertime. I've got to get a little sleep every now and then."

"Boss," Hubert said, "I wouldn't never wake you up at all, not at any time, but Miss Willie just sits there high up on the steps showing her pretty and that white man has been out there whittling on a little stick a long time without saying nothing. I'm scared about something happening when he whittles that little stick clear through, and it's just about whittled down to nothing now. That's why I waked you up, Mr. Vic. Ain't much left of that little whittling-stick."

Vic glanced again at Willie, and from her he turned to stare at the stranger sitting under the water-oak tree in his front yard.

The piece of wood had been shaved down to paper thinness.

"Boss," Hubert said, shifting the weight of his body uneasily, "we ain't aiming to have no trouble today, is we?"

"Which way did he come from?" Vic asked, ignoring the question.

"I never did see him come from nowhere, Mr. Vic. I just looked up, and there he was, sitting against the water oak out yonder and whittling on that little stick. I reckon I must have been drowsy when he came, because when I opened my eyes, there he was."

Vic slid down over the quilt until his legs were hanging over the edge of the porch. Perspiration began to trickle down his neck as soon as he sat up.

"Ask him what he's after, Hubert."

"We ain't aiming to have no trouble today, is we, Mr. Vic?"

"Ask him what he wants around here," he said.

Hubert went almost halfway to the water-oak tree and stopped.

"Mr. Vic says what can he do for you, white-folks?"

The man said nothing. He did not even glance up from the little stick he was whittling.

Hubert came back to the porch, the white of his eyes becoming larger with each step.

"What did he say?" Vic asked him.

"He ain't said nothing yet, Mr. Vic. He acts like he don't hear me at all. You'd better go talk to him, Mr. Vic. He won't give me no attention. Appears to me like he's just sitting there and looking at Miss Willie on the high step. Maybe if you was to tell her to go in the house and shut the door, he might be persuaded to give some notice to what we say to him."

"Ain't no sense in sending her in the house," Vic said. "I can make him talk. Hand me that stillyerd."

"Mr. Vic, I'm trying to tell you about Miss Willie. Miss Willie's been sitting there on that high step showing her pretty and he's been looking at her a right long time, Mr. Vic. If you won't object to me saying so, Mr. Vic, I reckon I'd tell Miss Willie to go sit somewhere else, if I was you. Miss Willie ain't got much on today, Mr. Vic. Just only that skimpy outside dress, Mr. Vic. That's what I've been trying to tell you. I walked out there in the yard this while ago to see what he was looking at so much, and when I say Miss Willie ain't got much on today, I mean she's got on just only that skimpy outside dress, Mr. Vic. You can go look yourself and see if I'm lying to you, Mr. Vic."

"Hand me that stillyerd, I said."

Hubert went to the end of the porch and brought the heavy iron cotton-weighing steelyard to Vic. He stepped back out of the way.

"Boss," Hubert said, "we ain't aiming to have no trouble today, is we?"

Vic was getting ready to jump down into the yard when the man under the water oak reached into his pocket and pulled out another knife. It was about ten or eleven inches long, and both sides of the handle were covered with hairy cowhide. There was a spring button in one end. The man pushed the button with his thumb, and the blade sprang from the case. He began playing with both knives, throwing them up into the air and catching them on the backs of his hands.

Hubert moved to the other side of Vic.

"Mr. Vic," he said, "I ain't intending to mess in your business none, but it looks to me like you got yourself in for a peck of trouble when you went off and brought Miss Willie back here. It looks to me like she's got up for a city girl, more so than a country girl."

Vic cursed him.

"I'm telling you, Mr. Vic, you ought to marry yourself a wife who hadn't ought to sit on a high step in front of a stranger, not even when she's wearing something more than just only a skimpy outside dress. I walked out there and looked at Miss Willie, and, Mr. Vic, Miss Willie is as bare as a plucked chicken, except for one little place I saw."

"Shut up," Vic said, laying the steelyard down on the quilt beside him.

The man under the water oak closed the blade of the small penknife and put it into his pocket. The big hairy cowhide knife he flipped into the air and caught it easily on the back of his hand.

"Mr. Vic," Hubert said, "you've been asleep all the time and you don't know like I do. Miss Willie has been sitting there on that high step showing off her pretty a long time now, and he's got his pecker up. I know, Mr. Vic, because I went out there myself and looked."

Vic cursed him.

The man in the yard flipped the knife into the air and caught it behind his back.

"What's your name?" he asked Willie.

"Willie."

He flipped the knife again.

"What's yours?" she asked him, giggling.

"Floyd."

"Where are you from?"

"Carolina."

He flipped it higher than ever, catching it underhanded.

"What are you doing in Georgia?"

"Don't know," he said. "Just looking around."

Willie giggled, smiling at him.

Floyd got up and walked across the yard to the steps and sat down on the bottom one. He put his arms around his knees and looked up at Willie.

"You're not so bad-looking," he said. "I've seen lots worse-looking."

"You're not so bad yourself," Willie giggled, resting her arms on her knees and looking down at him.

"How about a kiss?"

"What would it be to you?"

"Not bad. I reckon I've had lots worse."

"Well, you can't get it sitting down there."

Floyd climbed the steps on his hands and feet and sat down on the next to the top step. He leaned against Willie, putting one arm around her waist and the other under her knees. Willie slid down the step beside him. Floyd pulled her to him, making a sucking sound with his lips.

"Boss," Hubert said, his lips twitching, "we ain't aiming to have no trouble today, is we?"

Vic cursed him.

Willie and Floyd moved down a step without loosening their embrace.

"Who is that yellow-headed sapsucker, anyhow?" Vic said. "I'll be dadburned if he ain't got a lot of nerve — coming here and fooling with Willie."

"You wouldn't do nothing to cause trouble, would you, Mr. Vic? I surely don't want to have no trouble today, Mr. Vic."

Vic glanced at the eleven-inch knife Floyd had stuck into the step at his feet. It stood on its tip, twenty-two inches high, while the sun was reflected against the bright blade and made a streak of light on Floyd's pants leg.

"Go over there and take that knife away from him and bring it to me," Vic said. "Don't be scared of him."

"Mr. Vic, I surely hate to disappoint you, but if you want that white-folk's knife, you'll just have to get it your own self. I don't aim to have myself all carved up with that thing. Mr. Vic, I surely can't accommodate you this time. If you want that white-folk's knife, you'll just be bound to get it your own self, Mr. Vic."

Vic cursed him.

Hubert backed away until he was at the end of the porch. He kept looking behind him all the time, looking to be certain of the exact location of the sycamore stump that was between him and the pine grove on the other side of the cotton field.

Vic called to Hubert and told him to come back. Hubert came slowly around the corner of the porch and stood a few feet from the quilt where Vic was sitting. His lips quivered and the whites of his eyes grew larger. Vic motioned for him to come closer, but he would not come an inch farther.

"How old are you?" Floyd asked Willie.

"Fifteen."

Floyd jerked the knife out of the wood and thrust it deeper into the same place.

"How old are you?" she asked him.

"About twenty-seven."

"Are you married?"

"Not now," he said. "How long have you been?"

"About three months," Willie said.

"How do you like it?"

"Pretty good so far."

"How about another kiss?"

"You just had one."

"I'd like another one now."

"I ought not to let you kiss me again."

"Why not?"

"Men don't like girls who kiss too much."

"I'm not that kind."

"What kind are you?"

"I'd like to kiss you a lot."

"But after I let you do that, you'd go away."

"No, I won't. I'll stay for something else."

"What?"

"To get the rest of you."

"You might hurt me."

"It won't hurt."

"It might."

"Let's go inside for a drink and I'll show you."

"We'll have to go to the spring for fresh water."

"Where's the spring?"

"Just across the field in the grove."

"All right," Floyd said, standing up. "Let's go."

He bent down and pulled the knife out of the wood. Willie ran down the steps and across the yard. When Floyd saw that she was not going to wait for him, he ran after her, holding the knives in his pocket with one hand. She led him across the cotton field to the spring in the pine grove. Just before they got there, Floyd caught her by the arm and ran beside her the rest of the way.

"Boss," Hubert said, his voice trembling, "we ain't aiming to have no trouble today, is we?"

Vic cursed him.

"I don't want to get messed up with a heap of trouble and maybe get my belly slit open with that big hairy knife. If you ain't got objections, I reckon I'll mosey on home now and cut me a little firewood for the cookstove."

"Come back here!" Vic said. "You stay where you are and stop making moves to go off."

"What is we aiming to do, Mr. Vic?"

Vic eased himself off the porch and walked across the yard to the water oak. He looked down at the ground where Floyd had been sitting, and then he looked at the porch step where Willie had been. The noonday heat beat down through the thin leaves overhead and he could feel his mouth and throat burn with the hot air he breathed.

"Have you got a gun, Hubert?"

"No, sir, boss," Hubert said.

"Why haven't you?" he said. "Right when I need a gun, you haven't got it. Why don't you keep a gun?"

"Mr. Vic, I ain't got no use for a gun. I used to keep one to shoot rabbits and squirrels with, but I got to thinking hard one day, and I traded it off the first chance I got. I reckon it was a good thing I traded, too. If I had kept it, you'd be asking for it like you did just now."

Vic went back to the porch and picked up the steelyard and hammered the porch with it. After he had hit the porch four or five times, he dropped it and stared out in the direction of the spring. He walked as far as the edge of the shade and stopped. He stook listening for a while.

Willie and Floyd could be heard down near the spring. Floyd said something to Willie, and Willie laughed loudly. There was silence again for several minutes, and then Willie laughed again. Vic could not tell whether she was crying or laughing. He was getting ready to turn and go back to the porch when he heard her cry out. It sounded like a scream, but it was not exactly that; it sounded like a shriek, but it wasn't that, either; it sounded more like someone laughing and crying simultaneously in a high-pitched, excited voice.

"Where did Miss Willie come from, Mr. Vic?" Hubert asked. "Where did you bring her from?"

"Down below here a little way," he said.

Hubert listened to the sounds that were coming from the pine grove.

"Boss," he said after a little while, "it appears to me like you didn't go far enough away."

"I went far enough," Vic said. "If I had gone any farther, I'd have been in Florida."

The colored man hunched his shoulders forward several times while he smoothed the white sand with his broad-soled shoes.

"Mr. Vic, if I was you, the next time I'd surely go that far, maybe farther."

"What do you mean, the next time?"

"I was figuring that maybe you wouldn't be keeping her much longer than now, Mr. Vic."

Vic cursed him.

Hubert raised his head several times and attempted to see down into the pine grove over the top of the growing cotton.

"Shut up and mind your own business," Vic said. "I'm going to keep her till the cows come home. Where else do you reckon I'd find a better-looking girl than Willie?"

"Boss, I wasn't thinking of how she looks — I was thinking of how she acts. That white man came here and sat down and it wasn't no time before she had his pecker up."

"She acts that way because she ain't old enough yet to know who to fool with. She'll catch on in time."

Hubert followed Vic across the yard. While Vic went towards the porch, Hubert stopped and leaned against the water oak where he could almost see over the cotton field into the pine grove. Vic went up on the porch and stretched out on the quilt. He took off his shoes and flung them aside.

"I surely God knowed something was going to happen when he whittled that stick down to nothing," Hubert was saying to himself. "White-folks take a long time to whittle a little piece of wood, but when they whittle it down to nothing, they're going to be up and doing before the time ain't long."

Presently Vic sat upright on the quilt.

"Listen here, Hubert—"

"Yes, sir, boss!"

"You keep you eye on that stillyerd so it will stay right where it is now, and when they come back up the path, you wake me up in a hurry."

"Yes, sir, boss," Hubert said. "Are you aiming to take a little nap now?"

"Yes, I am. And if you don't wake me up when they come back, I'll break your neck for you when I do wake up."

Vic lay down again on the quilt and turned over on his side to shut out the blinding glare of the early afternoon sun that was reflecting upon the porch from the hard white sand in the yard.

Hubert scratched his head and sat down against the water oak, facing the path from the spring. He could hear Vic snoring on the porch above the sounds that came at intervals from the pine grove across the field. He sat staring down the path, drowsy, singing under his breath. It was a long time until sundown.

(First published in 1933 in *Esquire*)

The Picture

The first question John Nesbit asked Pauline when she told him that she had employed a new maid and nurse for the children, was the same thing he had always said when another servant came to take the place of one that had left.

"Pauline, what kind of a — are you sure that she is a good Negress?"

"She is a splendid housemaid, John, and she knows how to care for the children. Both Jay and Claire love her, and they obey her to the last word. She had the best recommendations of any servant we've ever hired. Mamie is the kind of maid I have wanted ever since we were married."

"Yes, I know," John said; "but is this new maid a good Negress?"

"Her recommendations were perfect, John. I haven't any reason to suspect her of not being a suitable nurse for the children."

"Well, you have seen her, and I haven't. I'd much rather not have a servant in the house than to employ one who wasn't a good Negress. I've seen too many of them at the plantation, when I was a kid growing up, to have one of that kind in the house."

"Don't worry about Mamie, John," Pauline said. "I'm sure she is a good girl. If she isn't, we can always ask her to leave."

That settled the matter for the rest of the evening. The next afternoon, though, when he reached home from the mills, John saw the new maid on the lawn with Jay and Claire. He drove his car into the garage and walked down the driveway to the side entrance. Just before he reached the steps he looked back over his shoulder at the colored girl sitting on the bench under the cedar trees. Both Jay and Claire had left Mamie and were running to meet him. He had a second chance to look at the girl before the children reached him.

Mamie was a brown girl with straightened hair. She had the slender body of a young woman, and her long legs were straight and round-looking in the ash-colored stockings that covered them above her knees. John had noticed all that about her when he looked at her for the first time over his shoulder. When he looked the second time, he saw that Mamie was full-breasted.

After the children had become tired of climbing over his lap and had gone back outdoors to play on the lawn with their nurse, John asked Pauline again about the colored girl. John was the agent at the Glen Rock Cotton Mills, and he had grown to be unrelenting in questioning every man and woman to whom he gave employment. He expected Pauline to be the same about the colored servants she hired for the house.

"I saw that new nurse just now," he said.

"Don't you think she's all right?" she asked.

"That's for you to be certain about, Pauline. You have the opportunity of knowing her. Is she a good Negress? We certainly don't wish to have the other kind to nurse Jay and Claire. It would be better for us not to have any servants at all, than to have the kind that we do not want in the house."

"I wish you wouldn't worry so much about Mamie, John. I just know that she is all right. Please stop worrying about it. Leave her to me. If I find out that she is not a good girl, I'll discharge her. When you come home from the mills you should rest, and not let yourself be worried about the servants."

"I know I should, Pauline," he said, "but you don't know the colored people as I do. You were raised in the East, where the only colored people are the ones who are probably as good as the whites, but down here in Carolina it's different, and you haven't lived here long enough yet to be able to distinguish between the two kinds. I was raised on a plantation with colored people, and I grew up in a small town where more than half the population was colored. I know there are two kinds of them, just as you know there are at least two distinct classes of whites. The reason I ask about the servants as I do is that I want to be sure that you do not let them fool you. We wouldn't want the wrong kind of servants in the house caring for Jay and Claire."

"Of course, we don't," Pauline said. "Now, let's forget about that. We must get ready for dinner soon. There isn't much time left for us to dress. Don't forget, we have an eight o'clock invitation."

Neither of them mentioned the new maid or the cook for several days. Pauline believed that John was assured at last that Mamie was a good Negress.

Less than a week later, though, something happened. Pauline missed one morning the silver-framed photograph of John that had been on the dressing table in her room since the day they were married. Once each week, on Tuesday, Pauline had cleaned the silver frame with cloth and paste, and on this Tuesday she could not find the picture anywhere in the house. She was not certain how long it had been missing from the table, because she had not consciously noticed it since Sunday. On Sunday she had dusted the silver and glass, and had put the silver-mounted photograph back on her dressing table. But on Tuesday it was missing.

The moment she realized that the picture was missing, she ran to the phone to call up John at his office at the mills. But while the operator was connecting them she suddenly realized that telling John about the picture was the last thing she should do. She hung up hurriedly, hoping that he would not suspect that it was she calling. She sat beside the telephone, her hands gripped together, waiting for the bell to ring. After five minutes she got up and ran from the room.

Pauline's first thought after leaving the room was, what in the world would John say to her if he should notice that the picture was missing! Suppose he should go to her room that evening after dinner and see that the photograph was not on her dressing table! He would surely ask her about it — what on earth could she tell him! She ran from room to room, looking over every inch of space in the house for the silver-framed photograph, and when she had finished, she was still as helpless as she had been the moment that she discovered it was missing. The picture was not in the house. Pauline was certain of that. She had searched everywhere.

Della, the cook, was not there at that time of the afternoon, and it was Mamie's day off. If they had been there she would have run to them and asked if they had seen Mr. Nesbit's photograph. She would even have asked them if either had taken it and put it some place else. But there was no one there then except herself and the children. It did not occur to her to ask Jay and Claire if they had taken the photograph without permission. They were then in the playhouse on the lawn.

She called to Jay and Claire as she ran to the garage for her car. Seating them beside her, she backed out the automobile, turned around in the driveway, and drove out into the boulevard. Pauline did not know where she was going until she had driven several blocks down the boulevard. It was then that she realized she had turned the car towards the Negro quarter, and that in a short time she would be there.

Pauline passed Della's house without giving it more than a glance. After she had passed Della's she wondered why she had not stopped there to ask Della if she had seen Mr. Nesbit's photograph that had always been on the dressing table in her bedroom.

A block and a half farther down the street was Mamie's house. Mamie lived there with her mother, Aunt Sophie, and several older brothers and sisters.

Pauline slowed down her car before she could see the house, and by the time she had reached it she had only to coast to a stop to jump out on the sandy sidewalk. Mamie's house looked very much like most of the other houses in the Negro quarter, but Pauline had seen it once before, and she needed only to recognize the ivy-trellised porch to tell her that it was the place where Mamie lived.

Several colored people were standing on the sidewalk, leaning against the whitewashed picket fence. None of them knew her, and Pauline did not stop to speak. She ran through the gate, up the steps to the open door. She knocked on the door as rapidly as she could. She could not wait much longer. John would be coming home from the mills at four o'clock, and it was past three o'clock then. There was not a minute to lose. She had to hurry.

Someone in the rear of the house opened a door and closed it. The delay made Pauline frantic. She took several steps into the hall, listening for somebody to answer her knocking.

Pauline was in the center of the hall when Mamie opened a bedroom door and came out.

"Why! Miss Pauline!" Mamie said, astonished. "What's the matter, Miss Pauline?"

"Mamie, I came to ask—"

She stopped in the midst of her questioning and could go no further. Mamie had crossed the hall and was standing a few feet from her. Pauline sat down in a chair and looked at Mamie. Her heart was beating madly, and her head throbbed until she had to hold her hands over her face to ease the pain.

"Miss Pauline, ask me what? What's happened to you, Miss Pauline? You look scared, Miss Pauline."

Pauline opened her eyes slowly and looked at Mamie. She saw now exactly what John must have seen when he saw Mamie for the first time nearly two weeks before. She could see that Mamie was young and slender, that her hair was straight and glistening, and that her mixed blood had given her a kind of sensuous beauty that no white girl could ever possess. She saw that Mamie's legs were long and slender, and that Mamie was full-breasted. It was only then that she fully realized what John had meant when he asked her if Mamie was a good Negress. She could answer him now. She knew what to tell John the next time he asked her that about one of the colored servants.

"Mamie, I came to ask if you know —"

The door behind Mamie had been left open, and she looked into the bedroom for the first time. The sunshine came into the room, and a light breeze whipped the white curtains. The bedroom dresser was in full view.

Without waiting to finish what she was about to say, Pauline jumped from the chair and ran into Mamie's room. There on the dresser, just as it had sat on her own dressing table, was John's silver-framed photograph. She snatched the picture in her arms and ran back to Mamie.

"What made you — why — when did you take it — what did you do it for, Mamie!"

Mamie smiled. She did not try to run away, nor did she attempt to defend herself. She smiled.

Pauline leaned against the wall, hugging the silver-framed photograph to her breast. Her head had stopped throbbing, but she felt too weak to stand any longer. Just in time, Mamie ran and brought the chair to her mistress.

Outside in the back yard a group of Negroes were talking, and, as suddenly as she had first heard their voices, they began to laugh. They were not laughing about something that was humorous. That would be another kind of laughter; white-folks' laughing, Aunt Sophie called it. The laughter that now came from their throats was different from any other expression of emotion Pauline had ever heard. They were not laughing at anything nor with anyone; they were laughing as only Negroes can laugh about nothing.

Pauline did not know how long she had been there in Mamie's house when she opened her eyes. She felt as though she had been in a deep sleep for hours. The laughter in the back yard had stopped, but echoes of it rolled in her head, just as the smile on Mamie's face had been only the beginning. She knew then that she could never forget what she had seen and heard in a Negro's house. She knew she would never be able to explain it to John, nor would she ever be able to explain the smile on Mamie's face, and the laughter in Aunt Sophie's back yard.

The silence in the house frightened her, and she realized how late it was in the afternoon. Pauline knew that John was at home wondering where she and the children were. She jumped to her feet unsteadily and ran through the doorway. Mamie ran beside her, holding her arm and supporting her with her other arm around her waist. They got into the car and sped homeward, with Mamie on the rear seat beside Jay and Claire.

John was standing on the porch when she turned into the driveway from the boulevard. She stopped her car and ran to him.

"Where have you been?" he asked, kissing her.

"Hold me tight, John! Hold me till it hurts!"

For several minutes she lay in his arms, her eyes closed, and her body trembling. It was only when he put his hand under her chin and raised her head that she could look into his eyes.

"Why is Mamie here this afternoon, Pauline?" he asked her. "I thought this was her day off."

"It was her day off, John, but I couldn't get along without her. I went to her house and brought her back."

She knew the question that he had asked dozens of times was about to be asked of her again. She knew the question was coming, because he had always asked it of her. While she waited, she lowered her head again, tightening her arms around his neck, and closed her eyes tightly.

"Are you sure that we wish to keep Mamie?" he asked her. "Pauline, is she a good Negress?"

"Yes, John," she said, her body relaxing in his arms. "Mamie is a good girl."

(First published in 1932 in the *New English Weekly*)

Yellow Girl

Nell stood at the kitchen window packing the basket of eggs. She arranged eleven white eggs carefully, placing the cottonseed hulls between them and under them so that none would be broken. The last one to be put into the basket was large and brown and a little soiled. She dipped it into the pan of soap and warm water and wiped it dry with a fresh dish towel. Even then she was not pleased with the way it looked, because it was brown; all the other eggs in the basket were as white as September cotton bolls.

Behind her in the room, Myrtie was scouring the two frying pans with soap water and a cloth dipped in sand. Nell laid down the brown egg and called Myrtie.

"Here's another of those big brown eggs, Myrtie," she said, pointing at the egg. "Do you have any idea where they come from? Have you seen any strange hens in the yard? There must be a visiting hen laying eggs in the chicken house."

Myrtie laid down the frying pan and came over to the little table by the window. She picked up the large brown egg and looked at it. The egg no longer looked brown. Nell looked at the egg again, wondering why in Myrtie's hands it had apparently changed color.

"Where do these brown eggs come from, Myrtie?" she asked. "There was one last week, and now today there's this. It was in the basket Mr. Willis brought in from the chicken house, but he said he forgot to notice which nest he took it from."

Myrtie turned the egg over in her hands, feeling the weight of it and measuring its enormous circumference with her fingers.

"Don't ask me, Miss Nell," Myrtie said, staring at the egg. "I've never seen a flock of Leghorns yet, though, that didn't lay a few brown eggs, sometime or other. Looks like it just can't be helped."

"What do you mean, Myrtie? What on earth are you talking about? Of course Leghorns lay white eggs; this is a brown egg."

"I'm not saying the Leghorns lay them, Miss Nell, and I'm not saying they don't. Those old Buff Orpingtons and Plymouth Rocks and Domineckers lay funny-looking eggs, too, sometimes. I wouldn't take on so much about finding one measly brown egg, though. I've never seen anybody yet, white or colored, who knew how such things happen. But I wouldn't worry about it, Miss Nell. Brown eggs are just as good as white eggs, to my way of tasting."

Nell turned her back on Myrtie and looked out the window until the girl had returned to the other side of the kitchen. Nell disliked to talk to Myrtie, because Myrtie pretended never to know the truth about anything. Even if she did know, she would invariably evade a straightforward answer. Myrtie would begin talking, and talk about everything under the sun from morning to night, but she would never answer a question that she could evade. Nell always forgave her, though; she knew Myrtie was not consciously evading the truth.

While the girl was scouring the pans, Nell picked up the egg again and looked at it closely. Mrs. Farrington had a flock of Dominique chickens, and she gathered in her chicken house eggs of all sizes, shapes, and colors. But that was to be expected, Mrs. Farrington had said, because she had two old roosters that were of no known name or breed. Nell had told Mrs. Farrington that some of her Dominiques were mixed-bred, and consequently they produced eggs of varying sizes, shapes, and colors; but Mrs. Farrington continued to lay all the blame on her two roosters, because, she said, they were a mixture of all breeds.

Once more Nell dipped the brown egg into the pan of water and wiped it with the fresh dish towel, but the egg remained as brown as it was at first. The egg was clean by then, but soap and water would not alter its size or change its color. It was a brown egg, and it would remain brown. Nell gave up, finally; she realized that she could never change it in any way. If she had had another egg to put into the basket in its place, she would have laid it aside and substituted a white one; but she only had a dozen, counting the brown one, and she wished to have enough to make an even exchange with Mrs. Farrington when she went over after some green garden peas.

Before she finally placed the egg in the basket with the others she glanced out the window to see where Willis was. He was sitting in the crib door shelling red seed corn into an old wooden lard pail.

"I'm going over to Mrs. Farringon's now to exchange these eggs for some peas," she told Myrtie. "Keep the fire going good, and put on a pan of water to boil. I'll be back in a little while."

She turned around and looked at Myrtie.

"Suppose you mash the potatoes today, for a change, Myrtie. Mr. Willis likes them that way."

"Are you going to take that big egg, Miss Nell?" Myrtie asked, looking down at it in the basket with the eleven white Leghorns.

"Certainly," she said. "Why?"

"Mrs. Farrington will be surprised to see it in with all those white ones, won't she, Miss Nell?"

"Well, what if she does see it?" Nell asked impatiently.

"Nothing, Miss Nell," Myrtie said. "But she might want to know where it came from. She knows we've got Leghorn hens, and she might think one of her Domineckers laid it."

"I can't help that," Nell said, turning away. "And, besides, she should keep her Dominiques at home if she doesn't want them to lay eggs in somebody else's chicken house."

"That's right, Miss Nell," Myrtie said. "She sure ought to do that. She ought to keep her Domineckers at home."

Nell was annoyed by the girl's comments. It was none of Myrtie's business, anyway. Myrtie was getting to be impertinent, and she was forgetting that she was a hired servant in the house. Nell left the kitchen determined to treat Myrtie more coldly after that. She could not allow a colored cook to tell her what to do and what not to do.

Willis was sitting in the crib door shelling the red seed corn. He glanced up when Nell came down the back steps, and looked at her. He stopped shelling corn for a moment to wipe away the white flakes of husk that clung to his eyes.

"I'm going over to Mrs. Farrington's now and exchange a basket of eggs for some green peas, Willis," she said. "I'll not be gone long."

"Maybe she won't swap with you today," Willis said. He stopped and looked up at her through the thin cloud of flying husk that hovered around him. "How do you know she will want to take eggs for peas today, Nell?"

"Don't be foolish, Willis," she said, smiling at him; "why wouldn't she take eggs in exchange today?"

"She might get to wondering where that big brown egg came from," he said, laughing. "She might think it is an egg one of her hens laid."

Nell stopped, but she did not turn around. She waited, looking towards the house.

"You're as bad as Myrtie, Willis."

"In which way is that?"

The moment he spoke, she turned quickly and looked at him. He was bending over to pick up an ear of seed corn.

"I didn't mean to say that, Willis. Please forget what I said. I didn't mean anything like that."

"Like what?"

"Nothing," she said, relieved. "It wasn't anything; I've even forgotten what it was I said. Good-by."

"Good-by," he said, looking after her, wondering.

Nell turned and walked quickly out of the yard and went around the corner of the house towards the road. The Farrington house was half a mile away, but by taking the path through the cotton field it was two or three hundred yards nearer. She crossed the road and entered the field, walking quickly along the path with the basket of eggs on her arm.

Halfway to the Farringtons' Nell turned around and looked back to see if Willis was still sitting in the crib door shelling seed corn. She did not know why she stopped and looked back, but even though she could not see him there or anywhere else in the yard, she went on towards the Farringtons' without thinking of Willis again.

Mrs. Farrington was sitting on the back porch peeling turnips when Nell turned the corner of the house and walked across the yard. There was a bucket of turnips beside Mrs. Farrington's rocking chair, and long purple peelings were lying scattered on the porch floor around her, twisted into shapes like apple peelings when they were tossed over the shoulder. Nell ran up the steps and picked up the longest peeling she could find; she picked up the peeling even before she spoke to Mrs. Farrington.

"Sakes alive, Nell," Mrs. Farrington said; "why are you throwing turnip peelings over your shoulder? Doesn't that good-for-nothing husband of yours love you any more?"

Nell dropped the turnip peeling, and, picking it up again, tore it into short pieces and threw them into the bucket. She blushed and sat down in the chair beside Mrs. Farrington.

"Of course, he loves me," Nell said. "I suppose I did that so many times when I was a little girl that I still have the habit."

"You mean it's because you haven't grown up yet, Nell," the woman said, chuckling to herself. "I used to be just like that myself; but, sakes alive, it doesn't last, always, girl."

Both of them laughed, and looked away, one from the other. Over across the cotton field a cloud of white dust hung close to the earth. Mr. Farrington and the colored men were planting cotton, and the earth was so dry it rose up in the air when it was disturbed by the mules' hooves and the cotton planters. There was no wind to carry the dust away, and it hung over the men and mules, hiding them from sight.

Presently Mrs. Farrington dropped a peeled turnip into the pan and folded her hands in her lap. She looked at Nell, noting her neatly combed hair and her clean gingham frock and white hands. Mrs. Farrington turned away again after that and gazed once more at the cloud of dust where her husband was at work.

"Maybe you and Willis will always be like that," she said. "Seems like you and Willis are still in love with each other. As long as he stays at home where he belongs and doesn't run off at night, it's a pretty sure sign he isn't getting ready to chase after another woman. Sakes alive, men can't always be depended upon to stay at home at night, though; they go riding off when you are least looking for them to."

Nell sat up, startled by what Mrs. Farrington had said, terrified by the directness of her comments.

"Of course, Willis wouldn't do a thing like that," she said confidently. "I know he wouldn't. Willis wouldn't do a thing like that. That's impossible, Mrs. Farrington."

Mrs. Farrington glanced at Nell, and then once more she looked across the field where the planting was being done. The cloud of white dust followed the men and mules, covering them.

"Seems like men are always saying something about being compelled to go to Macon on business, and even up to Atlanta sometimes," she said, ignoring Nell. "And then there are the times when they say they have to go to town at night. Seems like they are always going off to town at night."

Several Dominique hens came from under the porch and stopped in the yard to scratch on the hard white sand. They scratched listlessly; they went through the motions of scratching as if they knew of nothing else to do. They bent their long necks and looked down at the chicken-scrawls they had made with their claws, and they walked away aimlessly, neither surprised nor angry at not having unearthed a worm to devour. One of them began singing in the heat, drooping her wings until the tips of them dragged on the sand. The other hens paid no attention to her, strolling away without interest in the doleful music.

"You have pretty chickens, Mrs. Farrington," Nell said, watching the Dominiques stroll across the yard and sit down in the shaded dust holes as though they were nests.

"They're nothing but Domineckers," she said; "sakes alive, a body can't call them much of a breed, but they do get around to laying an egg or two once in a while."

Nell glanced down at the basket of eggs in her lap, covering the brown egg with her hand. She looked quickly at Mrs. Farrington to see if she had noticed what she had done.

"How are your Leghorns laying now, Nell?" she asked.

"Very well. Willis gathered sixteen eggs yesterday."

"My Domineckers seem to be taking a spell of resting. I only gathered two eggs yesterday, and that's not enough for a hungry man and a yard full of blacks. Sakes alive, we were saying only last night that we wished you would bring over some eggs in a day or two. And now here you are with them. Half an hour's prayer couldn't have done better."

"I thought you might let me have some green peas for dinner," Nell said, lifting the basket and setting it on the floor. "Willis likes green peas at this time of year, and ours haven't begun to bear yet."

"You're as welcome to as many as you want," Mrs. Farrington said. "Just walk into the kitchen, Nell, and look on the big table and you'll find a bushel basket of them. Help yourself to all you think you and Willis will want. We've got more than we can use. Sakes alive, there'll be another bushel ready for picking tomorrow morning, too."

Nell went into the kitchen and placed the eleven Leghorn eggs and the big brown one in a pan. She filled the basket with green peas and came back to the porch, closing the screen noiselessly behind her.

"Sit down, Nell," Mrs. Farrington said, "and tell me what's been happening. Sakes alive, I sit here all day and never hear a word of what's going on."

"Why, I haven't heard of anything new," Nell said.

"What's Willis doing now?"

"He's getting ready to plant corn. He was shelling the seed when I left home. He should be ready to begin planting this afternoon. The planter broke down yesterday, and he had to send to Macon for a new spoke chain. It should be here in the mail today."

"Myrtie is still there to help you with the house, isn't she?"

"Yes, Myrtie is still there."

The hens lying in the dust holes in the shade of the sycamore tree stood up and flapped their wings violently, beating the dust from their feathers. They stretched, one leg after the other, and flapped their wings a second time. One of them spread her legs, bending her knees as if she were getting ready to squat on the ground, and scratched the hard white sand five or six times in quick succession. The other hens stood and watched her while she stretched her long neck and looked down at the marks she had made; and then, wiping her beak on her leg as one whets a knife blade, she turned and waddled back across the yard and under the porch out of sight. The other hens followed her, singing in the heat.

"Couldn't you find a black woman to help you with the house?" Mrs. Farrington asked.

"A black woman?" Nell said. "Why, Myrtie is colored."

"She's colored all right," Mrs. Farrington said; "but, sakes alive, Nell, she isn't black. Myrtie is yellow."

"Well, that's all right, isn't it?" Nell asked. "Myrtie is yellow, and she is a fairly good cook. I don't know where I could find a better one for the pay."

"I reckon I'd heap rather have a black girl and a poor cook, than to have a yellow girl and the finest cook in the whole country."

Nell glanced quickly at Mrs. Farrington, but her head was turned, and she did not look at Nell.

There was a long silence between them until finally Nell felt that she must know what Mrs. Farrington was talking about.

One of the Dominiques suddenly appeared on the bottom step. She came hopping up to the porch, a step at a time. When she reached the last one, Mrs. Farrington said, "Shoo!" The hen flew to the yard and went back under the porch.

"You don't mean —"

Mrs. Farrington began rocking slowly, backward and forward. She gazed steadily across the field where her husband was planting cotton with the colored men.

"You don't mean Willis and —"

One of the roosters strutted across the yard, his eye first upon the hens under the porch and next upon the two women, and stopped midway in the yard to stand and fix his eye upon Mrs. Farrington and Nell. He stood jerking his head from side to side, his hanging scarlet comb blinding his left eye, while he listened to the squeaking of Mrs. Farrington's chair. After a while he continued across the yard and went out of sight behind the smoke-house.

"Mrs. Farrington, Willis wouldn't do anything like that!" Nell said indignantly.

"Like what?" Mrs. Farrington asked. "Sakes alive, Nell, I didn't say he would do anything."

"I know you didn't say it, Mrs. Farrington, but I thought you said it. I couldn't help thinking that you did say it."

"Well, that's different," she replied, much relieved. "I wouldn't want you to go telling Willis I did say it. Menfolks never understand what a woman means, anyway, and when they are told that a woman says something about them, they sometimes fly off the handle something awful."

Nell got up and stood beside the chair. She wished she could run down the steps and along the path towards home without another second's delay, but she knew she could not jump up and leave Mrs. Farrington like that, after what had been said. She would have to pretend that she was not in such a great hurry to get home.

"You're not going so soon, are you, Nell? Why, sakes alive, it seems like you only got here two or three minutes ago, Nell."

"I know," she said, "but it's getting late, and I've got to go home and get these peas ready for dinner. I'll be back to see you soon."

She walked carelessly down the steps. Mrs. Farrington got up and followed her across the hard yard. When they reached the beginning of the path that led across the field, Mrs. Farrington stopped. She never went any farther than that.

"I'm afraid I must hurry home now and hull the peas in time for dinner," Nell said, backing down the path. "I'll be back again in a few days, Mrs. Farrington. Thank you so much for the peas. Willis has wanted some for the past week or longer."

"It's as fair an exchange as I can offer for the Leghorn eggs," she said, laughing. "Because if there's anything I like better than those white Leghorn eggs, I don't know what it is. I get so tired of eating my old Dominecker's brown eggs I sometimes say I hope I may never see another one. Maybe I'll be asking you for a setting of them some day soon."

"Good-by," Nell said, backing farther and farther away. She

turned and walked several steps. "I'll bring you another basket soon, Mrs. Farrington."

It seemed as if she would never reach the house, even though it was only half a mile away. She could not run, because Mrs. Farrington was in the yard behind her watching, and she could not walk slowly, because she had to get home as soon as possible. She walked with her eyes on the patch in front of her, forcing herself to keep from looking up at the house. She knew that if she did raise her eyes and look at it, she would never be able to keep herself from running. If she did that, Mrs. Farrington would see her.

It was not until she had at last reached the end of the patch that she was able to look backward. Mrs. Farrington had left her yard, and Nell ran across the road and around to the back of the house.

Willis was nowhere within sight. She looked first at the crib where she had hoped she would find him, but he was not there, and the crib door was closed and locked. She looked down at the barn, but he was not there, either. When she glanced hastily over the fields, she was still unable to see him anywhere.

She stopped at the bottom step on the back porch. There was no sound within the house that she could hear, and not even the sound of Myrtie's footsteps reached her ears. The place seemed to be entirely deserted, and yet she knew that could not be, because only half an hour before when she left to go to Mrs. Farrington's to exchange eggs, Willis was sitting in the crib door shelling seed corn, and Myrtie was in the kitchen scouring the two frying pans.

Nell's hands went out and searched for the railing that led up the porch steps. Her hands could not find it, and her eyes would not let her see it.

The thought of Mrs. Farrington came back to her again and again. Mrs. Farrington, sitting on her own back porch, talking. Mrs. Farrington, sitting in her rocking chair, looking. Mrs. Farrington, peeling purple-top turnips, talking about yellow girls.

Nell felt deathly sick. She felt as if she had been stricken with an illness that squeezed the core of her body. Deep down within herself, she was deathly ill. A pain that began by piercing her skull struck downward and downward until it became motionless in her stomach. It remained there, gnawing and biting, eating the organs of her body and drinking the flow of her blood. She sank limp and helpless upon the back porch steps. Although she did not know where she was, she could still see Mrs. Farrington. Mrs. Farrington, in her rocking chair, looking. Mrs. Farrington, peeling purple-top turnips, talking about yellow girls.

Nell did not know how much later it was when she opened her eyes. The day was the color of the red seed corn Willis had been shelling when she last saw him sitting in the crib door, and it swam in a sea so wide that she almost cried out in fear when she saw it. Slowly she remembered how she had come to be where she was. She got to her feet weakly, holding to the railing for support.

Stumbling up the steps and across the porch, she flung open the screen door and went into the kitchen. Myrtie was standing beside the table mashing the boiled Irish potatoes with a long fork that had seven tines. Myrtie looked up when Nell ran in, but she did not have an opportunity to speak. Nell ran headlong through the dining room and on into the front room. Myrtie looked surprised to see her running.

Nell paused a moment in the doorway, looking at Willis, at the room, at the daybed, at the floor, at the rugs, at the open door that led into their room. She stood looking at everything she could see. She looked at the pillows on the daybed, at the rugs on the floor, at the chairs against the wall, at the counterpane on their bed. Remembering, she looked at the carpet in their room. Willis sat in front of her reading the *Macon Telegraph* that had just come in the mail, and he was calmly smoking his pipe. She glanced once more at the daybed, at the pillows arranged upon it, and at the rug in front of it. Running, she went to their room and ran her hands over the counterpane of the bed. She picked up the pillows, feeling them, and laid them down again. She ran back into the other room where Willis was.

Willis looked up at her.

Nell ran and fell on her knees in front of him, forcing her body between his legs and locking her arms around him. She pressed her feverish face against his cool cheeks and closed her eyes tightly. She forced herself tightly to him, holding him with all her might.

"Did Mrs. Farrington exchange with you?" he asked. "I'll bet a pretty that she had something to say about that big brown egg in a basketful of Leghorns."

Nell felt her body shake convulsively, as if she were shivering with cold. She knew she had no control over herself now.

"Look here," he said, throwing aside the *Telegraph* and lifting her head and looking into her eyes. "I know where that brown egg came from now. I remember all about it. There was one of Mrs. Farrington's old Dominecker hens over here yesterday morning. I saw her scratching in the yard, and she acted like she didn't give a cuss whether she clawed up a worm or not. She would scratch awhile and then walk off without even looking to see if she had turned up a worm."

Nell felt herself shaking again, but she did not attempt to control herself. If she could only lie there close to Willis with her arms around him, she did not care how much she shivered. As long as she was there, she had Willis; when she got up and walked out of the room, she would never again be that certain.

(First published in 1933 in *Story*)

Picking Cotton

About an hour after sunrise every morning during the cotton-picking season, people began coming towards the Donnie Williams farm from all directions. They came walking over the fields from four and five miles away, following the drain ditches, wading waist-high through the brown broom sedge in the fallow land, and shuffling through the yellow road dust. They came in pairs, in families, and in droves.

There were nearly five hundred acres of cotton to gather, and the Williamses were paying fifty cents a hundred pounds. Besides that, though, there were good-sized watermelons for every man, woman, and child, both white and colored, at dinnertime. Everybody liked to pick cotton at the Donnie Williams place, even though some of the farmers who could not find enough hands were offering seventy-five a hundred pounds, and even up as high as a dollar a hundred. But none of them had free watermelons for everybody.

Even though everyone liked to pick cotton for Donnie Williams, it was unusual to find the same people in the fields for two consecutive days. A man, with his family, would work for Donnie a day, and then stay at home a day to pick his own crop, or to just lie around the house and rest. Then there were the drifters who never stayed at one farm longer than a day. They had no homes to go to at night, so they slept in field houses and went to the next farm the following day. There were always new pickers arriving, and usually there were just as many people coming as there were leaving.

It had become a custom at Donnie Williams's place for the pickers to work in pairs. Donnie had tried out all kinds of schemes to get his crop gathered as quickly as he could before the price began to fall, and he had found out that people could, and would, pick better if they worked in pairs. Sometimes, otherwise, when there were crowds of twenty and thirty together, all of them would stop picking to laugh at a joke, and stand up to talk with the others. Ten or fifteen minutes wasted of every hour cut down the number of pounds a man could gather in a day, and Donnie was trying to get his crop through the gins as soon as possible.

I sometimes paired off with a Negro boy named Sonny. He and I had a lot to talk about, because he worked as houseboy for Mrs. Williams when he was not needed in the fields, and he knew a lot that I was anxious to hear.

Three or four times I had paired off with a redheaded girl from across the country. Her name was Gertie. She was about fifteen, and she knew more riddles than anybody I ever saw. She used to ask me riddles all the time we were picking, and when I could not answer them and had to give up, she would sit down, lift her calico skirt, and fan her face with it while she laughed at me for not knowing the answers.

Once she asked me if I knew what was the age of consent. I was not certain that I did know.

"Come on and tell me, Gertie," I begged her.

"You think it over tonight, Harry," she said, "and if you don't know by tomorrow, I'll tell you."

Gertie had a habit of giggling when she asked me something like that, and now she was giggling again. All that time she was fanning her face with her skirt, drawing the calico higher and higher above her waist while she laughed at me.

"It's real funny," she giggled.

There was nothing funny to me about a riddle I could not answer, nor even guess, but no amount of begging would ever make Gertie tell me the answer to that one. She would always sit down on her cotton-bag, cross her slender round legs under her, and fan her face with her skirt while she giggled because I did not know what to say.

It was all right for her to do that if she wished to, but I was never able to pick much cotton and look at her naked from the waist down at the same time. She would sit there and giggle about the riddle, fanning herself furiously, and smile at me. It would even have been all right for her to sit down on her cotton-bag and lift her skirt like that if only she had worn something under the one-piece calico wrapper. As long as I knew Gertie though, she never did.

"Why does an old maid look under the bed at night before she puts out the light, Harry?"

"God damn it, Gertie!" I shouted at her. "Why don't you keep your dress down where it belongs!"

I could not pick cotton when she did like that, and it made me angry.

"You can make up good riddles, too, can't you, Harry?" she said.

I was just getting ready to jump over to her row and throw her down when I looked around and saw Donnie Williams walking across the field not far away, and I had to go back to work right away.

After picking with one of the Johnsons for two days, I again paired off one morning with Gertie. We started off at a fast pace, each of us trying his best to get ahead of the other. Gertie had thought up a lot of new riddles to ask me, but we were so busy trying to leave each other behind that she did not have time to say anything to me for several hours.

It was about dinnertime when I heard her whistle to me. I turned around to see what she wished.

"Harry," she said, straightening up and packing the cotton in her bag with her feet, "do you see that black-haired girl over there with the old woman?"

She pointed over the rows towards them.

"What about her?" I asked.

"She was paired off yesterday with that Dennis boy, and last night she weighed in four hundred pounds, and the boy had only fifty pounds."

"Hell, Gertie," I said, "that's no riddle. Can't you think up a better one than that? She's not the first to weigh in more than a man. You can see them stripping over in the broom sedge almost any time that Donnie's not around."

"I don't suppose she is," Gertie said, sitting down and fanning her face with the calico skirt, "because I weighed in three-fifty myself the other night when I was picking with Sonny. He didn't have much more than forty pounds at quitting time, either."

That made me angry. I threw off the strap over my shoulder and jumped over the row beside her.

"God damn you, Gertie," I shouted, grabbing her by the arms, "did you let that damn nigger —"

"Let him do what?" she asked, giggling a little and pulling her skirt above her waist. "Did I let him give me some of his cotton?"

"Yes —"

"Sonny gave me only a hundred pounds, Harry."

"I'm going to beat hell out of him," I told her. "He ought to have better sense than to pair off with a white girl. And anyway, he ought to have given you two hundred pounds —"

Gertie twisted her shoulders from side to side and her heavy breasts shook until I thought that they would surely burst.

"I've just thought of a good riddle, Harry!" she said, naked again from her waist down. "Listen to this: If Sonny offered me a hundred pounds and you offered me two hundred, which one of you would I rather have take me?"

"Any fool knows that two hundred is twice as much as one hundred, Gertie. And anyway, Sonny is a nigger!"

"When are you ever going to learn how to answer riddles, Harry?" she said, fanning herself faster and faster. "Two hundred is twice as much as one hundred, but you're not Sonny."

She had begun to giggle, but before she could laugh at me, I caught her and threw her down, and began stuffing cotton into her mouth.

"That damn nigger, Sonny, won't ever —"

I said that much, but I never finished saying all I had meant to tell her when I jumped on her. I could see by looking into her eyes that she had thought of a new riddle, and that as soon as I took the cotton from her mouth she would ask me another one that I could not answer.

(First published in 1932 in *Contempo*)

Wild Flowers

The mockingbird that had perched on the roof top all night, filling the clear cool air with its music, had flown away when the sun rose. There was silence as deep and mysterious as the flat sandy country that extended mile after mile in every direction. Yesterday's shadows on the white sand began to reassemble under the trees and around the fence posts, spreading on the ground the lacy foliage of the branches and the fuzzy slabs of the wooden fence.

The sun rose in leaps and bounds, jerking itself upward as though it were in a great hurry to rise above the tops of the pines so it could shine down upon the flat country from there to the Gulf.

Inside the house the bedroom was light and warm. Nellie had been awake ever since the mockingbird had left. She lay on her side with one arm under her head. Her other arm was around the head beside her on the pillow. Her eyelids fluttered. Then for a minute at a time they did not move at all. After that they fluttered again, seven or eight or nine times in quick succession. She waited as patiently as she could for Vern to wake up.

When Vern came home sometime late in the night, he did not wake her. She had stayed awake waiting for him as long as she could, but she had become so sleepy her eyes would not stay open until he came.

The dark head on the pillow beside hers looked tired and worn. Vern's forehead, even in sleep, was wrinkled a little over his nose. Around the corners of his eyes the skin was darker than it was anywhere else on his face. She reached over as carefully as possible and kissed the cheek closest to her. She wanted to put both arms around his head and draw him to her, and to kiss him time after time and hold his dark head tight against her face.

Again her eyelids fluttered uncontrollably.

"Vern," she whispered softly. "Vern."

Slowly his eyes opened, then quickly closed again.

"Vern, sweet," she murmured, her heart beating faster and faster.

Vern turned his face toward her, snuggling his head between her arm and breast, and moving until she could feel his breath on her neck.

"Oh, Vern," she said in a whisper.

He could feel her kisses on his eyes and cheek and forehead and mouth. He was comfortably awake by then. He found her with his hands and they drew themselves tightly together.

"What did he say, Vern?" she asked at last, unable to wait any longer. "What, Vern?"

He opened his eyes and looked at her, fully awake at last.

She could read what he had to say on his face.

"When, Vern?" she said.

"Today," he said, closing his eyes and snuggling his head into her warmth once more.

Her lips trembled a little when he said it. She could not help herself.

"Where are we going to move to, Vern?" she asked like a little girl, looking closely to his lips for his answer.

He shook his head, pushing it tightly against her breasts and closing his eyes against her body.

They both lay still for a long time. The sun had warmed the room until it was almost like summer again, instead of early fall. Little waves of heat were beginning to rise from the weatherworn windowsill. There would be a little more of summer before winter came.

"Did you tell him —?" Nellie said. She stopped and looked down at Vern's face. "Did you tell him about me, Vern?"

"Yes."

"What did he say?"

Vern did not answer her. He pushed his head against her breast and held her tighter, as though he were struggling for food that would make his body strong when he got up and stood alone in the bare room.

"Didn't he say anything, Vern?"

"He just said he couldn't help it, or something like that. I don't remember what he said, but I know what he meant."

"Doesn't he care, Vern?"

"I guess he doesn't, Nellie."

Nellie stiffened. She trembled for a moment, but her body stiffened as though she had no control over it.

"But you care what happens to me, don't you, Vern?"

"Oh, God, yes!" he said. "That's all I do care about now. If anything happens —"

For a long time they lay in each other's arms, their minds stirring them wider and wider awake.

Nellie got up first. She was dressed and out of the room before Vern knew how quickly time had passed. He leaped out of bed, dressed, and hurried to the kitchen to make the fire in the cookstove. Nellie was already peeling the potatoes when he got it going.

They did not say much while they ate breakfast. They had to move, and move that day. There was nothing else they could do. The furniture did not belong to them, and they had so few clothes it would not be troublesome to carry them.

Nellie washed the dishes while Vern was getting their things ready. There was nothing to do after that except to tie up his overalls and shirts in a bundle, and Nellie's clothes in another, and to start out.

When they were ready to leave, Nellie stopped at the gate and looked back at the house. She did not mind leaving the place, even though it had been the only home she and Vern had ever had together. The house was so dilapidated that probably it would fall down in a few years more. The roof leaked, one side of the house had slipped off the foundation posts, and the porch sagged all the way to the ground in front.

Vern waited until she was ready to leave. When she turned away from the house, there were tears in her eyes, but she never looked back at it again. After they had gone a mile, they had turned a bend in the road, and the pines hid the place from sight.

"Where are we going, Vern?" she said, looking at him through the tears.

"We'll just have to keep on until we find a place," he said. He knew that she knew as well as he did that in that country of pines and sand the farms and houses were sometimes ten or fifteen miles apart. "I don't know how far that will be."

While she trudged along the sandy road, she could smell the fragrance of the last summer flowers all around her. The weeds and scrub hid most of them from sight, but every chance she got she stopped a moment and looked along the side of the ditches for blossoms. Vern did not stop, and she always ran to catch up with him before she could find any.

In the middle of the afternoon they came to a creek where it was cool and shady. Vern found her a place to lie down and, before taking off her shoes to rest her feet, scraped a pile of dry pine needles for her to lie on and pulled an armful of moss from the trees to put under her head. The water he brought her tasted of the leaves and grasses in the creek, and it was cool and clear. She fell asleep as soon as she had drunk some.

It was late afternoon when Vern woke her up.

"You've been asleep two or three hours, Nellie," he said. "Do you think you could walk a little more before night?"

She sat up and put on her shoes and followed him to the road. She felt a dizziness as soon as she was on her feet. She did not want to say anything to Vern about it, because she did not want him to worry. Every step she took pained her then. It was almost unbearable at times, and she bit her lips and crushed her fingers in her fists, but she walked along behind him, keeping out of his sight so he would not know about it.

At sundown she stopped and sat down by the side of the road. She felt as though she would never be able to take another step again. The pains in her body had drawn the color from her face, and her limbs felt as though they were being pulled from her body. Before she knew it, she had fainted.

When she opened her eyes, Vern was kneeling beside her, fanning her with his hat. She looked up into his face and tried to smile.

"Why didn't you tell me, Nellie?" he said. "I didn't know you were so tired."

"I don't want to be tired," she said. "I just couldn't help it, I guess."

He looked at her for a while, fanning her all the time.

"Do you think it might happen before we get some place?" he asked anxiously. "What do you think, Nellie?"

Nellie closed her eyes and tried not to think. They had not passed a house or farm since they had left that morning. She did not know how much farther it was to a town, and she was afraid to think how far it might be even to the next house. It made her afraid to think about it.

"I thought you said it would be another two weeks . . .?" Vern said. "Didn't you, Nellie?"

"I thought so," she said. "But it's going to be difficult now, walking like this all day."

His hat fell from his hand, and he looked all around in confusion. He did not know what to do, but he knew he had to do something for Nellie right away.

"I can't stand this," he said. "I've got to do something."

He picked her up and carried her across the road. He found a place for her to lie under a pine tree, and he put her down there. Then he untied their bundles and put some of their clothes under her head and some over her feet and legs.

The sun had set, and it was becoming dark. Vern did not know what to do next. He was afraid to leave her there all alone in the woods, but he knew he had to get help for her.

"Vern," she said, holding out her hand to touch him.

He grasped it in his, squeezing and stroking her fingers and wrist.

"What is it, Nellie?"

"I'm afraid it is going to happen . . . happen . . . happen right away," she said weakly, closing her eyes before she could finish.

He bent down and saw that her lips were bloodless and that her face was whiter than he had ever seen anyone's face. While he watched her, her body became tense and she bit her mouth to keep from screaming with pain.

Vern jumped up and ran to the road, looking up it and down it. The night had come down so quickly that he could not tell whether there were any fields or cleared ground there as an indication of somebody's living near. There were no signs of a house or people anywhere.

He ran back to Nellie.

"Are you all right?" he asked her.

"If I could go to sleep," she said, "I think I would be all right for a while."

He got down beside her and put his arms around her.

"If I thought you wouldn't be afraid, I'd go up the road until I found a house and get a car or something to carry you. I can't let you stay here all night on the ground."

"You might not get back — in time!" she cried frantically.

"I'd hurry as fast as I could," he said. "I'll run until I find somebody."

"If you'll come back in two or three hours," she said, "I'd be able to stand it, I think. I couldn't stand it any longer than that alone, though."

He got up.

"I'm going," he said.

He ran up the road as fast as he could, remembering how he had pleaded to be allowed to stay in the house a little longer so Nellie would not have to go like that. The only answer he had got, even after he had explained about Nellie, was a shake of the head. There was no use in begging after that. He was being put out, and he could not do anything about it. He was certain there should have been some money due him for his crop that fall, even a few dollars, but he knew there was no use in trying to argue about that, either. He had gone home the night before, knowing they would have to leave. He stumbled, falling heavily, headlong, on the road.

When he picked himself up, he saw a light ahead. It was only a pale ray from a board window that had been closed tightly. But it was a house, and somebody lived in it. He ran toward it as fast as he could.

When he got to the place, a dog under the house barked, but he paid no attention to it. He ran up to the door and pounded on it with both fists.

"Let me in!" he yelled. "Open the door!"

Somebody inside shouted, and several chairs were knocked over. The dog ran out from under the house and began snapping at Vern's legs. He tried to kick the dog away, but the dog was just as determined as he was, and came back at him more savagely than before. Finally he pushed the door open, breaking a button lock.

Several Negroes were hiding in the room. He could see heads and feet under the bed and behind a trunk and under a table.

"Don't be scared of me," he said as calmly as he could. "I came for help. My wife's down the road, sick. I've got to get her into a house somewhere. She's lying on the ground."

The oldest man in the room, a gray-haired Negro who looked about fifty, crawled from under the bed.

"I'll help you, boss," he said. "I didn't know what you wanted when you came shouting and yelling like that. That's why I didn't open the door and let you in."

"Have you got a cart, or something like that?" Vern asked.

"I've got a one-horse cart," the man said. "George, you and Pete go hitch up the mule to the cart. Hurry and do it."

Two Negro boys came from their hiding places and ran out the back door.

"We'll need a mattress, or something like that to put her on," Vern said.

The Negro woman began stripping the covers from the bed, and Vern picked up the mattress and carried it out the front door to the road. While he waited for the boys to drive the cart out, he walked up and down, trying to assure himself that Nellie would be all right.

When the cart was ready, they all got in and drove down the road as fast as the mule could go. It took less than half an hour for them to reach the grove where he had left Nellie, and by then he realized he had been gone three hours or longer.

Vern jumped to the ground, calling her. She did not answer. He ran up the bank and fell on his knees beside her on the ground.

"Nellie!" he said, shaking her. "Wake up, Nellie! This is Vern, Nellie!"

He could not make her answer. Putting his face down against hers, he felt her cold cheek. He put his hands on her forehead, and that was cold, too. Then he found her wrists and held them in his fingers while he pressed his ear tightly against her breast.

The Negro man finally succeeded in pulling him backward. For a while he did not know where he was or what had happened. It seemed as if his mind had gone completely blank.

The Negro was trying to talk to him, but Vern could not hear a word he was saying. He did know that something had happened, and that Nellie's face and hands were cold, and that he could not feel her heart beat. He knew, but he could not make himself believe that it was really true.

He fell down on the ground, his face pressed against the pine needles, while his fingers dug into the soft damp earth. He could hear voices above him, and he could hear the words the voices said, but nothing had any meaning. Sometime — a long time away — he would ask about their baby — about Nellie's — about their baby. He knew it would be a long time before he could ask anything like that, though. It would be a long time before words would have any meaning in them again.

(First published in 1938 in *Southways*)

The Mortal Sickness
Of a Mind . . .

The Negro in the Well

Jule Robinson was lying in bed snoring when his foxhounds struck a live trail a mile away and their baying woke him up with a start. He jumped to the floor, jerked on his shoes, and ran out into the front yard. It was about an hour before dawn.

Holding his hat to the side of his head like a swollen hand, he listened to the trailing on the ridge above the house. With his hat to deflect the sound into his ear, he could hear the dogs treading in the dry underbrush as plainly as his own breathing. It had taken him only a few seconds to determine that the hounds were not cold-trailing, and he put his hat back on his head and stooped over to lace his shoes.

"Papa," a frightened voice said, "please don't go off again now — wait till daybreak, anyway."

Jule turned around and saw the dim outline of his two girls. They were huddled together in the window of their bedroom. Jessie and Clara were old enough to take care of themselves, he thought, but that did not stop them from getting in his way when he wanted to go fox hunting.

"Go on back to bed and sleep, Jessie — you and Clara," he said gruffly. "Those hounds are just up on the ridge. They can't take me much out of hollering distance before sunup."

"We're scared, Papa," Clara said.

"Scared of what?" Jule asked impatiently. "There ain't a thing for two big girls like you and Jessie to be scared of. What's there to be scared of in this big country, anyway?"

The hounds stopped training for a moment, and Jule straightened up to listen to the silence. All at once they began again, and he bent down to finish tying his shoes.

Off in the distance he could hear several other packs of trailing hounds, and by looking closely at the horizon he could see the twinkle of campfires where bands of fox hunters had stopped to warm their hand and feet.

"Are you going, anyway, Papa?" Clara asked.

"I'm going, anyway," he answered.

The two girls ran back to bed and pulled the covers over their heads. There was no way to argue with Jule Robinson when he had set his head on following his foxhounds.

The craze must have started anew sometime during the holidays, because by the end of the first week in January it looked and sounded as if everybody in Georgia were trading foxhounds by day and bellowing "Whoo-way-ho!" by night. From the time the sun went down until the next morning when it came up, the woods, fields, pastures, and swamps were crawling with beggar-liced men and yelping hound-dogs. Nobody would have thought of riding horseback after the hounds in a country where there was a barbwire fence every few hundred yards.

Automobiles roared and rattled over the rough country roads all night long. The fox hunters had to travel fast in order to keep up with the pack.

It was not safe for any living thing with four legs to be out after sundown, because the hounds had the hunting fever too, and packs of those rangy half-starved dogs were running down and devouring calves, hogs, and even yellow-furred bobcats. It had got so during the past two weeks that the chickens knew enough to take to their roosts an hour ahead of time, because those packs of gaunt hunt-hungry hounds could not wait for sunset any more.

Jule finished lacing his shoes and went around the house. The path to the ridge began in the back yard and weaved up the hillside like a cowpath through a thicket. Jule passed the well and stopped to feel in his pockets to see if he had enough smoking tobacco to last him until he got back.

While he was standing there he heard behind him a sound like water gurgling through the neck of a demijohn. Jule listened again. The sound came even more plainly while he listened. There was no creek anywhere within hearing distance, and the nearest water was in the well. He went to the edge and listened again. The well did not have a stand or a windlass; it was merely a twenty-foot hole in the ground with boards laid over the top to keep pigs and chickens from falling into it.

"O Lord, help me now!" a voice said.

Jule got down on his hands and knees and looked at the well cover in the darkness. He felt of the boards with his hands. Three of them had been moved, and there was a black oblong hole that was large enough to drop a calf through.

"Who's that?" Jule said, stretching out his neck and cocking his ear.

"O Lord, help me now," the voice said again, weaker than before.

The gurgling sound began again, and Jule knew then that it was the water in the well.

"Who's down there muddying up my well?" Jule said.

There was no sound then. Even the gurgling stopped.

Jule felt on the ground for a pebble and dropped it into the well. He counted until he could hear the *kerplunk* when it struck the water.

"Doggone your hide, whoever you are down there!" Jule said. "Who's down there?"

Nobody answered.

Jule felt in the dark for the water bucket, but he could not find it. Instead, his fingers found a larger pebble, a stone almost as big around as his fist, and he dropped it into the well.

The big rock struck something else before it finally went into the water.

"O Lord, I'm going down and can't help myself," the voice down there said. "O Lord, a big hand is trying to shove me under."

The hounds trailing on the ridge swung around to the east and started back again. The fox they were after was trying to back-trail them, but Jule's hounds were hard to fool. They had got to be almost as smart as a fox.

Jule straightened up and listened to the running.

"Whoo-way-oh!" he called after the dogs.

That sent them on yelping even louder than before.

"Is that you up there, Mr. Jule?" the voice asked.

Jule bent over the well again, keeping one ear on the dogs on the ridge. He did not want to lose track of them when they were on a live trail like that.

"This is me," Jule said. "Who's that?"

"This is only Bokus Bradley, Mr. Jule," the voice said.

"What you doing down in my well, muddying it up like that, Bokus?"

"It was something like this, Mr. Jule," Bokus said. "I was coming down the ridge a while ago, trying to keep up with my hounds, and I stumbled over your well cover. I reckon I must have missed the path, somehow or other. Your well cover wouldn't hold me up, or something, and the first thing I knew, here I was. I've been here ever since I fell in. I reckon I've been down here most of the night. I hope you ain't mad at me, Mr. Jule. I just naturally couldn't help it at all."

"You've muddied up my well water," Jule said. "I ain't so doggone pleased about that."

"I reckon I have, some," Bokus said, "but I just naturally couldn't help it none at all."

"Where'd your dogs go to, Bokus?" Jule asked.

"I don't know, Mr. Jule. I haven't heard a sound out of them since I fell in here. They was headed for the creek when I was coming down the ridge behind them. Can you hear them anywhere now, Mr. Jule?"

Several packs of hounds could be heard. Jule's on the ridge was trailing east, and a pack was trailing down the creek toward town. Over toward the hills several more packs were running, but they were so far away it was not easy to tell to whom they belonged.

"Sounds to me like I hear your dogs down the creek, headed for the swamp," Jule said.

"Whoo-way-oh!" Bokus called.

The sound from the well struck Jule like a blast out of a megaphone.

"Your dogs can't hear you from 'way down there, Bokus," he said.

"I know they can't, Mr. Jule, and that's why I sure enough want to get out of here. My poor dogs don't know which way I want them to trail when they can't hear me talk to them. Whoo-way-oh!" Bokus shouted. "O Lord, help me now!"

Jule's dogs sounded as if they were closing in on a fox, and Jule jumped. "Whoo-way-oh!"

"Is you still up there, Mr. Jule?" Bokus asked. "Please, Mr. Jule, don't go away and leave me down here in this cold well. I'll do anything for you if you'll just only get me out of here. I've been standing neck-deep in this cold water near about all night long."

Jule threw some of the boards over the well.

"What you doing up there, Mr. Jule?"

Jule took off his hat and held the brim like a fan to the side of his head. He could hear the panting of the dogs while they ran.

"How many foxhounds have you got, Bokus?" Jule asked.

"I got me eight," Bokus said. "They're mighty fine fox trailers, too, Mr. Jule. But I'd like to get me out of this here well before doing much more talking with you."

"You could get along somehow with less than that, couldn't you, Bokus?"

"If I had to, I'd have to," Bokus said, "but I sure enough would hate to have fewer than my eight dogs, though. Eight is just naturally the rightsized pack for me, Mr. Jule."

"How are you figuring on getting out of there?" Jule said.

"I just naturally figured on you helping me out, Mr. Jule," he said. "Leastaways, that's about the only way I know of getting out of this here well. I tried climbing, but the dirt just naturally crumbles away every time I dig my toes into the sides."

"You've got that well so muddied up it won't be fit to drink out of for a week or more," Jule said.

"I'll do what I can to clean it out for you, Mr. Jule, if I ever get up on top of the solid ground again. Can you hear those hounds of mine trailing now, Mr. Jule?"

"They're still down the creek. I reckon I could lower the water bucket, and I could pull a little, and you could climb a little, and maybe you'd get out that way."

"That just naturally would suit me fine, Mr. Jule," Bokus said eagerly. "Here I is. When is you going to lower that water bucket?"

Jule stood up and listened to his dogs trailing on the ridge. From the way they sounded, it would not be long before they treed the fox they were after.

"It's only about an hour till daybreak," Jule said. "I'd better go on up the ridge and see how my hounds are making out. I can't do much here at the well till the sun comes up."

"Don't go away and leave me now, Mr. Jule," Bokus begged. "Mr. Jule, please, sir, just lower that water bucket down here and help me get out. I just naturally got to get out of here, Mr. Jule. My dogs will get all balled up without me following them. Whoo-way-oh! Whoo-way-oh!"

The pack of fox-trailing hounds was coming up from the creek, headed toward the house. Jule took off his hat and held it beside his ear. He listened to them panting and yelping.

"If I had two more hounds, I'd be mighty pleased," Jule said, shouting loud enough for Bokus to hear. "Just two is all I need right now."

"You wouldn't be wanting two of mine, would you, Mr. Jule?" Bokus asked.

"It's a good time to make a trade," Jule said. "It's a mighty good time, being as how you are down in the well and want to get out."

"Two, did you say?"

"Two is what I said."

There was silence in the well for a long time. For nearly five minutes Jule listened to the packs of dogs all around him, some on the ridge, some down the creek, and some in the far-off fields. The barking of the hounds was a sweeter sound to him than anything else in the world. He would lose a night's sleep any time just to stay up and hear a pack of foxhounds live-trailing.

"Whoo-way-oh!" he called.

"Mr. Jule!" Bokus shouted up from the bottom of the well.

Jule went to the edge and leaned over to hear what the Negro had to say.

"How about that there trade now, Bokus?"

"Mr. Jule, I just naturally couldn't swap off two of my hounds, I just sure enough couldn't."

"Why now?" Jule said.

"Because I'd have only just six dogs left, Mr. Jule, and I couldn't do much fox hunting with just that many."

Jule straightened up and kicked the boards over the top of the well.

"You won't be following even so few as one hound for a while," he said, "because I'm going to leave you down in the bottom where you stand now. It's another hour, almost, till daybreak, and I can't be wasting that time staying here talking to you. Maybe when I get back you'll be in a mind to do some trading, Bokus."

Jule kicked the boards on top of the well.

"O Lord, help me now!" Bokus said. "But, O Lord, don't make me swap off no two hounds for the help I'm asking for."

Jule stumbled over the water bucket when he turned and started across the yard toward the path up the ridge. Up there he could hear his dogs running again, and when he took off his hat and held it to the side of his head he could hear Polly pant, and Senator snort, and Mary Jane whine, and Sunshine yelp, and the rest of them barking at the head of the trail. He put on his hat, pulled it down hard all around, and hurried up the path to follow them on the ridge. The fox would not be able to hold out much longer.

"Whoo-way-oh!" he called to his hounds. "Whoo-way-oh!"

The echo was a masterful sound to hear.

(First published in 1935 in the *Atlantic Monthly*)

Runaway

Mrs. Garley was seated at the head of the table drinking coffee and reading the paper after breakfast when she heard a plate fall and break on the kitchen floor. The boarders had eaten and left, and she was alone in the room. Garley had left the house too.

When she ran to the kitchen door, threw it open, and looked inside at Lessie, the little Negro girl was cringing in the corner behind the range.

"So you broke another one of my dishes, did you?" Mrs. Garley said evenly. Her anger was slowly rising; the longer she stood and looked at Lessie, the madder she could become. "That makes two you've broken this month, Lessie. And that's two too many for me to stand for."

The nine-year-old colored girl moved inch by inch farther into the corner. She never knew what Mrs. Garley might do to her next.

"You come out here in the middle of this floor, Lessie," the woman said. "Come this minute when I speak to you!"

The girl came several steps, watching Mrs. Garley and trembling all over. When she was halfway to the center of the room, Mrs. Garley ran to her and slapped her on both sides of her face. The blows made her so dizzy she did not know where she was or what she was doing. She threw her arms around her head protectingly.

"You stinking little nigger!" Mrs. Garley shouted at her.

Before Lessie could run back to the corner behind the stove, Mrs. Garley snatched up the broom and began beating her with it, striking her as hard as she could over the head, shoulders, and on her back. The girl began to cry, and fell on the floor. Mrs. Garley struck her while she lay there screaming and writhing.

"Now, you get up from there and get to work cleaning this house," she told Lessie, putting the broom away. "I want every room in this house as clean as a pin by twelve o'clock."

She left the kitchen and went into the front of the house.

II

Lessie had complained about the work. She had complained about washing so many dishes and cleaning so many rooms in the boardinghouse. She said she was too tired to finish them every day. Mrs. Garley had slapped her for every word she uttered.

"If that nigger has run away," she told her husband, "I'll whip her until there's nothing left of her."

"You can't expect too much of her," Garley said. "She's not big enough to do much heavy work."

"You talk like you're taking up for her," his wife said. "I feed her, give her clothes, and keep her. If she won't be grateful of her own accord, I'll make her be grateful."

Lessie had run away, and Mrs. Garley knew she had. Mrs. Garley had been expecting it to happen for some time, but she believed she had frightened the girl enough to keep her there. Lessie had been brought into town from the country when she was four years old, and for the past three years she had done all the housework.

"It's about time to let her go, anyway," Garley said. "You wouldn't be able to keep her much longer without paying her something."

"There you go, taking up for her again! I pay her with her meals and bed. That's all she should have. I wouldn't give her a red cent besides that."

Garley shook his head, still not convinced. For one thing, he was afraid there might be trouble if they kept her any longer. Everybody in town knew they kept Lessie there to do the work, and somebody might want to make trouble for them. His wife worked the girl harder than a grown person.

"Well, I want Lessie back, and I want you to bring her back," his wife said. "I want her back by tomorrow morning at breakfast time."

Garley looked at his wife but said nothing. He depended upon her for his living. Without her and the boardinghouse, he did not know what he could do. She ran the boardinghouse and paid all the bills. When she told him to do something, he could not say he would not do it. He got up and went through the house to the back porch.

There was a small room behind the kitchen, only long enough and wide enough for a cot that had been cut in half for Lessie. There never had been much in the room, except the bed, and now there was nothing else there. Even the two or three dresses his wife had made for Lessie by cutting down some of her old clothes were gone. Garley looked under the cot, and found nothing there. Lessie had run away, and there was nothing to show that she might have intended coming back. She had taken all she possessed.

When Garley saw his wife half an hour later, she stopped him in the hall, hands on hips.

"Well?" she said. "Do you expect to find her hiding under a chair somewhere in the house?"

"Where can I look?" he asked. "How do I know which way she went?"

"How do I know?" Mrs. Garley said. "If I knew, I'd go there and find her myself. You find Lessie and bring her back here by breakfast time tomorrow morning, if you know what's good for you. If you don't . . . if you don't . . ."

Garley found his hat and went out the front door. He turned down the street in the direction of the Negro quarter of town. That was the only likely place for Lessie to be hiding, unless she had gone to the country.

III

As soon as he passed the first Negro house in the quarter, Garley had a feeling that everybody in the neighborhood was watching him from behind doors, windows, and corners of buildings. He turned, jerking his head around quickly, and tried to catch somebody looking at him. There was nobody to be seen anywhere. The place looked completely deserted.

"Lessie wouldn't know any of these darkies," he said to himself. "She never left home, and nobody ever came there to see her. I wouldn't be surprised if nobody knew she was alive, except my wife and me. Lessie wouldn't come down here among strangers when she ran away."

He walked on, trying to think where he could look for her. He decided she would not have gone to the country, because she would have been too afraid to do that. The only other place for her to be hiding, after all, was in the quarter. If he did find her, he believed he would come across her hiding behind some Negro woman who had taken her in.

Garley had half made up his mind to go back home and tell his wife he had looked through every house in the quarter without finding Lessie. But when he stopped and started back, he began to think what his wife would say and do. She might even take it into her head to turn him out of house and home if he went back without Lessie, or word of her.

Turning down an alley, he picked out a house at random. The door and the windows were open, but there was no sign of anyone's being there. There was not even smoke in the chimney.

Garley hesitated, and then went to the house next door.

He knocked and listened. There was no sound anywhere, even though there was a fire under a washpot in the yard. He stepped into the doorway and looked inside. In the corner of the room sat a large Negro woman, rocking unconcernedly to and fro in a chair. On her lap, all but hidden in the folds of her breasts, sat Lessie. The girl was clinging to the woman and burying her head deeper under the woman's arms.

"Hello, Aunt Gracie," Garley said, staring at them.

"What do you want down here, Mr. Garley?" Aunt Gracie asked stiffly.

"Just looking around," Garley said.

"Just looking around for what?" the woman asked.

"Well, Lessie, I guess."

"It won't do you a bit of good," Aunt Gracie said. "You'll just be wasting your time talking about it."

"I didn't know where she was, to tell the truth," he said.

"And it won't do you no good to know where she is, either," Aunt Gracie said, "because you can go tell that wife of yours that she's going to stay where she is at."

Garley sat down in a chair by the door. The Negro woman hugged Lessie all the tighter and rocked her back and forth. Lessie had not looked at him.

"To tell the truth," Garley said, "my wife has been pretty hard on Lessie for the past three or four years. She's been a little harder than she ought to have been, I guess."

"She won't be again," Aunt Gracie said. "Because the child's going to stay right here with me from now on. You white people ought to be ashamed of yourselves for treating darkies like you do. You know good and well it couldn't be right to make Lessie work for you all the time and not give her something more than a few old rags made over from your wife's clothes when she is done with them, and what scraps get left over from the kitchen."

Garley hoped Aunt Gracie would not begin next about the way his wife had slapped and beat Lessie with the broom. He hoped nobody knew about that.

"When you get home," Aunt Gracie said, "tell your wife I've got Lessie, and that I'm going to keep her. Tell her to come down here herself after her, if she dares to, but I don't reckon she will, because she knows what I'll say to her will make her ears burn red."

Garley got up, taking one more look at Lessie. He had never known she was so small before. Even though she was nine years old, she looked no larger than a six- or seven-year-old girl. He backed to the door, not saying a word.

Outside in the alley again, he turned towards home. It would soon be time for supper, and meals were served on time. He looked at his watch as he hurried up the street through the quarter. On the way he cut across a vacant lot, to make certain that he got there in plenty of time.

His wife was standing on the front porch.

"Well, did you find Lessie?" she demanded.

"She'll be back by breakfast time," Garley said. "You told me that was when she had to be back, didn't you?"

"That's what I said, and if she's not here then, you can get ready to do some stirring around for yourself."

"I'll do the best I can," he said, hurrying through the hall behind her to the dining room, where the boarders had already sat down at the table.

Garley slipped into the room and got into his seat unnoticed. He was just in time to get a helping from the first dish that was passed down his side of the table.

(First published in 1938 in *Southways*)

The People v. Abe Lathan, Colored

Uncle Abe was shucking corn in the crib when Luther Bolick came down from the big white house on the hill and told him to pack up his household goods and move off the farm. Uncle Abe had grown a little deaf and he did not hear what Luther said the first time.

"These old ears of mine is bothering me again, Mr. Luther," Uncle Abe said. "I just can't seem to hear as good as I used to."

Luther looked at the Negro and scowled. Uncle Abe had got up and was standing in the crib door where he could hear better.

"I said, I want you and your family to pack up your furniture and anything else that really belongs to you, and move off."

Uncle Abe reached out and clutched at the crib door for support.

"Move off?" Uncle Abe said.

He looked into his landlord's face unbelievingly.

"Mr. Luther, you don't mean that, does you?" Uncle Abe asked, his voice shaking. "You must be joking, ain't you, Mr. Luther?"

"You heard me right, even if you do pretend to be half deaf," Luther said angrily, turning around and walking several steps. "I want you off the place by the end of the week. I'll give you that much time if you don't try to make any trouble. And when you pack up your things, take care you don't pick up anything that belongs to me. Or I'll have the law on you."

Uncle Abe grew weak so quickly that he barely managed to keep from falling. He turned a little and slid down the side of the door and sat on the crib floor. Luther looked around to see what he was doing.

"I'm past sixty," Uncle Abe said slowly, "but me and my family works hard for you, Mr. Luther. We work as hard as anybody on your whole place. You know that's true, Mr. Luther. I've lived here, working for you, and your daddy before you, for all of forty years. I never mentioned to you about the share, no matter how big the crop was that I raised for you. I've never asked much, just enough to eat and a few clothes, that's all. I raised up a houseful of children to help work, and none of them ever made any trouble for you, did they Mr. Luther?"

Luther waved his arm impatiently, indicating that he wanted the Negro to stop arguing. He shook his head, showing that he did not want to listen to anything Uncle Abe had to say.

"That's all true enough," Luther said, "but I've got to get rid of half the tenants on my place. I can't afford to keep eight or ten old people like you here any longer. All of you will have to move off and go somewhere else."

"Ain't you going to farm this year, and raise cotton, Mr. Luther?" Uncle Abe asked. "I can still work as good and hard as anybody else. It may take me a little longer sometimes, but I get the work done. Ain't I shucking this corn to feed the mules as good as anybody else could do?"

"I haven't got time to stand here and argue with you," Luther said nervously. "My mind is made up, and that's all there is to it. Now, you go on home as soon as you finish feeding the mules and start packing the things that belong to you like I told you."

Luther turned away and started walking down the path toward the barn. When he got as far as the barnyard gate, he turned around and looked back. Uncle Abe had followed him.

"Where can me and my family move to, Mr. Luther?" Uncle Abe said. "The boys is big enough to take care of themselves. But me and my wife has grown old. You know how hard it is for an old colored man like me to go out and find a house and land to work on shares. It don't cost you much to keep us, and me and my boys raise as much cotton as anybody else. The last time I mentioned the shares has been a long way in the past, thirty years or more. I'm just content to work like I do and get some rations and a few clothes. You know that's true, Mr. Luther. I've lived in my little shanty over there for all of forty years, and it's the only home I've got. Mr. Luther, me and my wife is both old now, and I can't hire out to work by the day, because I don't have the strength any more. But I can still grow cotton as good as any other colored man in the country."

Luther opened the barnyard gate and walked through it. He shook his head as though he was not even going to listen any longer. He turned his back on Uncle Abe and walked away.

Uncle Abe did not know what to say or do after that. When he saw Luther walk away, he became shaky all over. He clutched at the gate for something to hold on it.

"I just can't move away, Mr. Luther," he said desperately. "I just can't do that. This is the only place I've got to live in the world. I just can't move off, Mr. Luther."

Luther walked out of sight around the corner of the barn. He did not hear Uncle Abe after that.

The next day, at a little after two o'clock in the afternoon, a truck drove up to the door of the three-room house where Uncle Abe, his wife, and their three grown sons lived. Uncle Abe and his wife were sitting by the fire trying to keep warm in the winter cold. They were the only ones at home then.

Uncle Abe heard the truck drive up and stop, but he sat where he was, thinking it was his oldest boy, Henry, who drove a truck sometimes for Luther Bolick.

After several minutes had passed, somebody knocked on the door, and his wife got up right away and went to see who it was.

There were two strange white men on the porch when she opened the door. They did not say anything at first, but looked inside the room to see who was there. Still not saying anything, they came inside and walked to the fireplace where Uncle Abe sat hunched over the hearth.

"Are you Abe Lathan?" one of the men, the oldest, asked.

"Yes, sir, I'm Abe Lathan," he answered, wondering who they were, because he had never seen them before. "Why do you want to know that?"

The man took a bright metal disk out of his pocket and held it in the palm of his hand before Uncle Abe's eyes.

"I'm serving a paper and a warrant on you," he said. "One is an eviction, and the other is for threatening to do bodily harm."

He unfolded the eviction notice and handed it to Uncle Abe. The Negro shook his head bewilderedly, looking first at the paper and finally up at the two strange white men.

"I'm a deputy," the older man said, "and I've come for two things — to evict you from this house and to put you under arrest."

"What does that mean — evict?" Uncle Abe asked.

The two men looked around the room for a moment. Uncle Abe's wife had come up behind his chair and put trembling hands on his shoulder.

"We are going to move your furniture out of this house and carry it off the property of Luther Bolick. Then, besides that, we're going to take you down to the county jail. Now, come on and hurry up, both of you."

Uncle Abe got up, and he and his wife stood on the hearth not knowing what to do.

The two men began gathering up the furniture and carrying it out of the house. They took the beds, tables, chairs, and everything else in the three rooms except the cookstove, which belonged to Luther Bolick. When they got all the things outside, they began piling them into the truck.

Uncle Abe went outside in front of the house as quickly as he could.

"White-folks, please don't do that," he begged. "Just wait a minute while I go find Mr. Luther. He'll set things straight. Mr. Luther is my landlord, and he won't let you take all my furniture away like this. Please, sir, just wait while I go find him."

The two men looked at each other.

"Luther Bolick is the one who signed these papers," the deputy said, shaking his head. "He was the one who got these court orders to carry off the furniture and put you in jail. It wouldn't do you a bit of good to try to find him now."

"Put me in jail?" Uncle Abe said. "What did he say to do that for?"

"For threatening bodily harm," the deputy said. "That's for threatening to kill him. Hitting him with a stick or shooting him with a pistol."

The men threw the rest of the household goods into the truck and told Uncle Abe and his wife to climb in the back. When they made no effort to get in, the deputy pushed them to the rear and prodded them until they climbed into the truck.

While the younger man drove the truck, the deputy stood beside them in the body so they could not escape. They drove out the lane, past the other tenant houses, and then down the long road that went over the hill through Luther Bolick's land to the public highway. They passed the big white house where he lived, but he was not within sight.

"I never threatened to harm Mr. Luther," Uncle Abe protested. "I never did a thing like that in my whole life. I never said a mean thing about him either. Mr. Luther is my boss, and I've worked for him ever since I was twenty years old. Yesterday he said he wanted me to move off his farm, and all I did was say that I thought he ought to let me stay. I won't have much longer to live, noway. I told him I didn't want to move off. That's all I said to Mr. Luther. I ain't never said I was going to try to kill him. Mr. Luther knows that as well as I do. You ask Mr. Luther if that ain't so."

They had left Luther Bolick's farm, and had turned down the highway toward the county seat, eleven miles away.

"For forty years I has lived here and worked for Mr. Luther," Uncle Abe said, "and I ain't never said a mean thing to his face or behind his back in all that time. He furnishes me with rations for me and my family, and a few clothes, and me and my family raise cotton for him, and I been doing that ever since I was twenty years old. I moved here and started working on shares for his daddy first, and then when he died, I kept right on like I have up to now. Mr. Luther knows I has worked hard and never answered him

back, and only asked for rations and a few clothes all this time. You
ask Mr. Luther."

The deputy listened to all that Uncle Abe said, but he did not
say anything himself. He felt sorry for the old Negro and his wife,
but there was nothing he could do about it. Luther Bolick had
driven to the courthouse early that morning and secured the
papers for eviction and arrest. It was his job to serve the papers
and execute the court orders. But even if it was his job, he could
not keep from feeling sorry for the Negroes. He didn't think that
Luther Bolick ought to throw them off his farm just because they
had grown old.

When they had stopped, the two white men began unloading
the furniture and stacking it beside the road. When it was all out
of the truck, the deputy told Uncle Abe's wife to get out. Uncle
Abe started to get out, too, but the deputy told him to stay where
he was. They drove off again, leaving Uncle Abe's wife standing in
a dazed state of mind beside the furniture.

"What are you going to do with me now?" Uncle Abe asked,
looking back at his wife and furniture in the distance.

"Take you to the county jail and lock you up," the deputy said.

"What's my wife going to do?" he asked.

"The people in one of those houses will probably take her in."

"How long is you going to keep me in jail locked up?"

"Until your case comes up for trial."

They drove through the dusty streets of the town, around the
courthouse square, and stopped in front of a brick building with
iron bars across the windows.

"Here's where we get out," the deputy said.

Uncle Abe was almost too weak to walk by that time, but he
managed to move along the path to the door. Another white man
opened the door and told him to walk straight down the hall until
he was told to stop.

Just before noon Saturday, Uncle Abe's oldest son, Henry, stood
in Ramsey Clark's office, hat in hand. The lawyer looked at the
Negro and frowned. He chewed his pencil for a while, then swung
around in his chair and looked out the window into the courthouse square. Presently he turned around and looked at Uncle

Abe's son.

"I don't want the case," he said. "I don't want to touch it."

The boy stared at him helplessly. It was the third lawyer he had gone to see that morning, and all of them had refused to take his father's case.

"There's no money in it," Ramsey Clark said, still frowning. "I'd never get a dime out of you niggers if I took this case. And, besides, I don't want to represent any more niggers at court. Better lawyers than me have been ruined that way. I don't want to get the reputation of being a 'nigger lawyer.'"

Henry shifted the weight of his body from one foot to the other and bit his lips. He did not know what to say. He stood in the middle of the room trying to think of a way to get help for his father.

"My father never said he was going to kill Mr. Luther," Henry protested. "He's always been on friendly terms with Mr. Luther. None of us ever gave Mr. Luther trouble. Anybody will tell you that. All the other tenants on Mr. Luther's place will tell you my father has always stood up for Mr. Luther. He never said he was going to try to hurt Mr. Luther."

The lawyer waved for him to stop. He had heard all he wanted to listen to.

"I told you I wouldn't touch the case," he said angrily, snatching up some papers and slamming them down on his desk. "I don't want to go into court and waste my time arguing a case that won't make any difference one way or the other, anyway. It's a good thing for you niggers to get a turn on the 'gang every once in a while. It doesn't make any difference whether Abe Lathan threatened Mr. Bolick, or whether he didn't threaten him. Abe Lathan said he wasn't going to move off the farm, didn't he? Well, that's enough to convict him in court. When the case comes up for trial, that's all the judge will want to hear. He'll be sent to the 'gang quicker than a flea can hop. No lawyer is going to spend a lot of time preparing a case when he knows how it's going to end. If there was money in it, it might be different. But you niggers don't have a thin dime to pay me with. No, I don't want the case. I wouldn't touch it with a ten-foot pole."

Henry backed out of Ramsey Clark's office and went to the jail.

He secured permission to see his father for five minutes.

Uncle Abe was sitting on his bunk in the cage looking through the bars when Henry entered. The jailer came and stood behind him at the cage door.

"Did you see a lawyer and tell him I never said nothing like that to Mr. Luther?" Uncle Abe asked the first thing.

Henry looked at his father, but it was difficult for him to answer. He shook his head, dropping his gaze until he could see only the floor.

"You done tried, didn't you, Henry?" Uncle Abe asked.

Henry nodded.

"But when you told the lawyers how I ain't never said a mean thing about Mr. Luther, or his daddy before him, in all my whole life, didn't they say they was going to help me get out of jail?"

Henry shook his head.

"What did the lawyers say, Henry? When you told them how respectful I've always been to Mr. Luther, and how I've always worked hard for him all my life, and never mentioned the shares, didn't they say they would help me then?"

Henry looked at his father, moving his head sideways in order to see him between the bars of the cage. He had to swallow hard several times before he could speak at all.

"I've already been to see three lawyers," he said finally. "All three of them said they couldn't do nothing about it, and to just go ahead and let it come up for trial. They said there wasn't nothing they could do, because the judge would give you a turn on the 'gang, anyway."

He stopped for a moment, looking down at his father's feet through the bars.

"If you want me to, I'll go see if I can find some lawyers to take the case. But it won't do much good. They just won't do anything."

Uncle Abe sat down on his bunk and looked at the floor. He could not understand why none of the lawyers would help him. Presently he looked up through the bars at his son. His eyes were fast filling with tears that he could not control.

"Why did the lawyers say the judge would give me a turn on the 'gang, anyway, Henry?" he asked.

Henry gripped the bars, thinking about all the years he had

seen his father and mother working in the cotton fields for Luther Bolick and being paid in rations, a few clothes, and a house to live in, and nothing more.

"Why did they say that for, Henry?" his father insisted.

"I reckon because we is just colored folks," Henry said at last. "I don't know why else they would say things like that."

The jailer moved up behind Henry, prodding him with his stick. Henry walked down the hall between the rows of cages toward the door that led to the street. He did not look back.

(First published in 1939 in *Esquire*)

Savannah River Payday

A quarter of a mile down the river the partly devoured carcasses of five or six mules that had been killed during the past two weeks by the heat and overwork at the sawmill, lay rotting in the mid-afternoon sun. Of the hundred or more buzzards hovering around the flesh, some were perched drowsily on the cypress stumps, and some were strutting aimlessly over the cleared ground. Every few minutes one of the buzzards, with a sound like wagon-rumble on a wooden bridge, beat the sultry air with its wings and pecked and clawed at the decaying flesh. Dozens of the vultures glided overhead hour after hour in monotonous circles.

The breeze that had been coming up the river since early that morning shifted to the east and the full stench of sun-rotted muleflesh settled over the swamp. The July sun blazed over the earth and shriveled the grass and weeds until they were as dry as crisp autumn leaves. A cloud of dense black smoke blew over from the other side of the river when somebody threw an armful of fat pine on the fire under the moonshine still.

Jake blew his nose on the ground and asked Red for a smoke. Red gave him a cigarette.

"What time's it now, Red?"

Red took his watch from his overalls pocket and showed it to Jake.

"Looks to me like it's about three o'clock," he told Red.

Red jerked the pump out of the dust and kicked at the punctured tire. The air escaped just as fast as he could pump it. There was nothing in the old car to patch the tube with.

Jake spat at the Negro's head on the running board and grabbed Red's arm.

"That nigger's stinkin' worse than them mules, Red. Let's run that tire flat so we can git to town and git shed of him. I don't like to waste time around that smell."

Red was open to any suggestion. The sweat had been running down his face and over his chest and wetting his breeches. He had been pumping for half an hour trying to get some air into the tire. It had been flat when they left the sawmill.

Jake cranked up the engine and they got in and started up the road towards town. It was three miles to town from the sawmill.

The old automobile rattled up the road through the deep yellow dust. The sun was so hot it made the air feel like steam when it was breathed into the lungs. Most of the water had leaked from the radiator, and the engine knocked like ten-pound hammers on an anvil. Red did not care about the noise as long as he could get where he was going.

Half a mile up the road was Hog Creek. When they got to the top of the hill Red shut off the engine. The car rolled down to the creek and stopped on the bridge.

"Git some water for the radiator, Jake," Red said. He reached in the back seat and pulled out a tin can for Jake to carry the water in.

Jake crawled out of the car and stretched his arm and legs. He wiped the sweat off his face with his shirttail.

"Don't hurry me," Jake said, leaning against the car. "Ain't no hurry for nothin'."

Red got tired holding the can. He threw it at Jake. Jake dodged it and the can rolled off the bridge down into the creek. Red propped his feet on the windshield and got ready to take a nap while Jake was going for the water.

Jake walked around to the other side of the car and looked at the Negro. The hot sun had swollen the lips until they curled over and touched the nose and chin. The Negro had tripped up that morning when he tried to get out of the way of a falling cypress tree.

"What's this nigger's name?" he asked Red.

"Jim somethin'," Red grunted, trying to sleep.

Jake turned the head over with his foot so he could see the face. He happened to think that he might have known him.

"God Almighty!" he said, shaking Red by the arm. "Hand me that monkey wrench quick, Red."

Red lifted up the back seat and found the monkey wrench. He got out and handed it to Jake.

"What's the matter, Jake? What's the matter with the nigger?"

Jake picked up a stick and pushed back the Negro's lips.

"Look at them gold teeth, Red," he pointed.

Red squatted beside the running board and tried to count the gold teeth.

"Here, Red, you take this stick and hold his mouth open while I knock off that gold."

Red took the stick and pushed the lips away from the teeth. Jake choked the monkey wrench halfway and tapped on the first tooth. He had to hit it about six or seven times before it broke off and fell on the bridge. Red picked it up and rubbed the dirt off on his overalls.

"How much is it worth, Jake?" he asked, bouncing the tooth in the palm of his hand trying to feel the weight.

"About two dollars," Jake said. "Maybe more."

Jake took the tooth and weighed it in his hand.

"Hold his mouth open and let me knock out the rest of them," Jake said. He picked up the monkey wrench and choked it halfway. "There's about three or four more, looks like to me."

Red pushed the Negro's lips away from the teeth while Jake hammered away at the gold. The sun had made the teeth so hot they burned his fingers when he picked them off the bridge.

"You keep two and give me three," Red said. "It's my car we're totin' him to town in."

"Like hell I will," Jake said. "I found them, didn't I? Well, I got the right to keep three myself if I want to."

Red jerked the monkey wrench off the running board and socked Jake on the head with it. The blow was only hard enough to stun him. Jake reeled around on the bridge like he was dead drunk and fell against the radiator. Red followed him up and socked him again. A ball of skin and hair fell in the dust. He took all the gold teeth and put them into his overalls pocket. Jake was knocked out cold. Red shook him and kicked him, but Jake didn't move. Red dragged him around to the back seat and threw him inside and shut the door. Then he cranked up the car and started to town. The tire that was punctured had dropped off the wheel somewhere down the road and there was nothing left except the rim to ride on.

Red had gone a little over a mile from the bridge when Jake came to himself and sat up on the back seat. He was still a little dizzy, but he knew what he was doing.

"Hold on a minute, Red," he shouted. "Stop this automobile."

Red shut off the engine and the car rolled to a stop. He got out in the road.

"What you want now, Jake?" he asked him.

"Look, Red," he pointed across the cotton field beside the road. "Look what's yonder, Red."

A mulatto girl was chopping cotton about twenty rows from the road. Red started across the field after her before Jake could get out. They stumbled over the cotton rows kicking up the plants with every step.

Jake caught up with Red before they reached the girl. When they were only two rows away, she dropped her hoe and started running towards the woods.

"Hey, there!" Jake shouted. "Don't you run off!"

He picked up a heavy sun-baked clod and heaved it at her as hard as he could. She turned around and tried to dodge it; but she could not get out of the way in time, and it struck her full on the forehead.

Red got to her first. The girl rubbed her head and tried to get up. He pushed her down again.

Jake came running up. He tried to kick her dress above her

waist with his foot.

"Wait a minute," Red said. He shoved Jake off his feet. "I got here first."

"That don't cut no ice with me," Jake said. He started for Red and butted him down. Then he stood over him and tried to stomp Red's head with his heels.

Red got away and picked up the girl's hoe and swung it with all his might at Jake's head. The sharp blade caught Jake on the right side of his head and sliced his ear off close to his face. Jake fell back and felt his face and looked at the ear on the ground.

Red turned around to grab the girl, but she was gone. She was nowhere in sight.

"Come on, Jake," he said. "She run off. Let's git to town and dump that nigger. I want 'bout a dozen good stiff drinks. I don't work all week and let payday git by without tankin' up good and plenty."

Jake tore one of the sleeves out of his shirt and made a bandage to tie around his head. It did not bleed so much after that.

Red went back to the car and waited for Jake. The dead Negro on the running board was a hell of a lot of trouble. If it had not been for him, the girl would not have got scared and run away.

They got into the car again and started to town. They had to get to the undertaker's before six o'clock, because he closed up at that time; and they did not want to have to carry the dead Negro around with them all day Sunday.

"What time's it now, Red?" Jake asked him.

Red pulled out his watch and showed it to Jake.

"Looks like it's about five o'clock," Jake told him.

Red put the watch back into his overalls pocket.

It was about a mile and a half to town yet, and there was a black cloud coming up like there might be a big thunderstorm. The old car had got hot again because they did not get the water at Hog Creek, and the engine was knocking so hard it could be heard half a mile away.

Suddenly the storm broke overhead and the water came down in bucketfuls. There was no place to stop where they could get out of the rain and there was no top on the car. Red opened the throttle as wide as it would go and tried to get to town in a hurry.

The rain cooled the engine and made the car run faster.

When they got to the edge of town, the old car was running faster than it ever had. The rain came down harder and harder all the time. It was a cloudburst, all right.

Then suddenly one of the cylinders went dead, and the machine slowed down a little. In a minute two more of the cylinders went dead at the same time, and the car could barely move on the one that was left. The rain would drown that one out, too, in a little while.

The car went as far as the poolroom and stopped dead. All the cylinders were full of water.

"Git out, Red," Jake shouted. "I'll bet you a quart of corn I can beat you five games of pool."

Red was right behind Jake. The rain had soaked every thread of their clothes.

The men in the poolroom asked Jake and Red where they got the Negro and what they were going to do with him.

"We're takin' him to the undertaker's when the shower's over," Red said. "He got tripped up down at the sawmill this mornin'. Right on payday, too."

Some of the hounds that were not too lazy went out in the rain and smelled the Negro on the running board.

One of the men told Jake he had better go to the drugstore and have his head fixed. Jake said he couldn't be bothered.

Jake beat Red the first four games, and then Red wanted to bet two quarts that he could win the last game. He laid a ragged five-dollar bill on the table, for a side bet. Jake covered that with a bill that was even more ragged.

Red had the break on the fifth game. He slammed away with his stick and lucked the eleven ball, the fifteen, the nine, and the four ball.

"Hell," Jake said, "I'll spot you that thirty-nine and beat you." He chalked his stick and got ready to make a run, after Red missed his next shot. "All I want is one good shot and I'll make game before I stop runnin' them. We shoot pool where I come from."

Jake made the one, two, three, and lucked the twelve ball. He chalked his cue again and got ready to run the five ball in.

Just as he was tapping the cue ball somebody on the other side of the table started talking out loud.

"He ain't no pool shot," the man laughed. "I bet he don't make that five ball."

Jake missed.

Before anybody knew what was happening, Jake had swung the leaded butt-end of his cue stick at the man's head with all his might. The man fell against another table and struck his head on a sharp-edged spittoon. A four-inch gash had been opened on his head by the stick, and blood was running through a crack in the floor.

"I'll teach these smart guys how to talk when I'm shootin' pool," Jake said. "I bet he don't open his trap like that no more."

The man was carried down to the doctor's office to get his head sewed up.

Red took two more shots and made game. Jake was ready to pay off.

They went out the back door and got the corn in a half-gallon jug. Jake took half a dozen swallows and handed the jug over to Red, Red drank till the jug was half full. Then they went back into the poolroom to shoot some more pool.

A man came running in from the street and told Jake and Red the marshal was outside waiting to see them.

"What does he want now?" Red asked him.

"He says he wants you-all to tote that nigger down to the undertaker's before he stinks the whole town up."

Jake took another half-dozen swallows out of the jug and handed it over to Red.

"Say," Jake said, falling against one of the tables, "you go tell that marshal that I said for him to take a long runnin' start and jump to hell. — Me and Red's shootin' pool!"

(First published in 1931 in *American Earth*)

Why Should Men Make Haste to Die?

The Fly in the Coffin

There was poor old Dose Muffin, stretched out on the corncrib floor, dead as a frostbitten watermelon vine in November, and a pesky housefly was walking all over his nose.

Let old Dose come alive for just one short minute, maybe two while about it, and you could bet your last sock-toe dollar that pesky fly wouldn't live to do his ticklish fiddling and stropping on any human's nose again.

"You, Woodrow, you!" Aunt Marty said. "Go look in that corncrib and take a look if any old flies worrying Dose."

"Uncle Dose don't care now," Woodrow said. "Uncle Dose don't care about nothing no more."

"Dead or alive, Dose cares about flies," Aunt Marty said.

There wasn't enough room in the house to stretch him out in. The house was full of people, and the people wanted plenty of room to stand around in. There was that banjo-playing fool in there, Hap Conson, and Hap had to have plenty of space when he was around. There was that jigging high-yellow gal everybody

called Goodie, and Goodie took all the room there was when she
histed up her dress and started shaking things.

Poor old Dose, dead a day and a night, couldn't say a word. That
old fly was crawling all over Dose's nose, stopping every now and
then to strop its wings and fiddle its legs. It had been only a day
and a night since Dose had chased a fly right through the buzz saw
at the lumber mill. That buzz saw cut Dose just about half in two,
and he died mad as heck about the fly getting away all well and
alive. It wouldn't make any difference to Dose, though, if he could
wake up for a minute, maybe two while about it. If he could only
do that, he would swat that pesky fly so hard there wouldn't be a
flyspeck left.

"You, Woodrow, you!" Aunt Marty said. "Go like I told you do
and see if any old flies worrying Dose."

"You wouldn't catch me swatting no flies on no dead man,"
Woodrow said.

"Don't swat them," Aunt Marty said. "Just shoo them."

Back the other side of the house they were trying to throw a
makeshift coffin together for Dose. They were doing a lot of
trying and only a little bit of building. Those lazybones out there
just didn't have their minds on the work at all. The undertaker
wouldn't come and bring one, because he wanted sixty dollars,
twenty-five down. Nobody had no sixty dollars, twenty-five down.

Soon as they got the coffin thrown together, they'd go and bury
poor old Dose, provided Dose's jumper was all starched and
ironed by then. The jumper was out there swinging on the
clothesline, waving in the balmy breeze, when the breeze came
that way.

Old Dose Muffin, lying tickle-nosed in the corncrib, was dead
and wanted burying as soon as those lazy, big-mouthed, good-for-
nothing sawmill hands got the grave dug deep enough. He could
have been put in the ground a lot sooner if that jabbering
preacher and that mushmouthed black boy would have laid aside
their jawboning long enough to finish the coffin they were trying
to throw together. Nobody was in a hurry like he was.

That time-wasting old Marty hadn't started washing out his
jumper till noon, and if he had had his way, she would have got up
and started at the break of day that morning. That banjo-playing

fool in the house there, Hap Conson, had got everybody's mind off the burial, and nobody had time to come out to the corncrib and swat that pesky fly on Uncle Dose's nose and say howdy-do. That skirt-histing high-yellow in there, Goodie, was going to shake the house down, if she didn't shake off her behind first, and there wasn't a soul in the world cared enough to stop ogling Goodie long enough to come out to the crib to see if any pesky flies needed chasing away.

Poor old Dose died a ragged-pants sawmill hand, and he didn't have no social standing at all. He had given up the best job he had ever had in his life, when he was porter in the white-folks' hotel, because he went off chasing a fly to death just because the fly lit on his barbecue sandwich just when he was getting ready to bite into it. He chased that fly eight days all over the country, and the fly wouldn't have stopped long enough then to let Dose swat him if it hadn't been starved dizzy. Poor old Dose came back home, but he had to go to work in the sawmill and lost all his social standing.

"You, Woodrow, you!" Aunt Marty said. "How many times does it take to tell you go see if any old flies worrying Dose?"

"I'd be scared to death to go moseying around a dead man, Aunt Marty," Woodrow said. "Uncle Dose can't see no flies no way."

"Dose don't have to be up and alive like other folks to know about flies," she said. "Dose sees flies, he dead or alive."

The jumper was dry, the coffin was thrown together, and the grave was six feet deep. They put the jumper on Dose, stretched him out in the box, and dropped him into the hole in the ground.

That jabbering preacher started praying, picking out the pine splinters he had stuck into his fingers when he and that mush-mouthed black boy were throwing together the coffin. That banjo-playing Hap Conson squatted on the ground, picking at the thing like it was red-hot coals in a tin pan. Then along came that Goodie misbehaving, shaking everything that wouldn't be still every time she was around a banjo-plucking.

They slammed the lid on Dose, and drove it down to stay with a couple of rusty twenty-penny nails. They shoveled in a few spades of gravel and sand.

"Hold on there," Dose said.

Marty was scared enough to run, but she couldn't. She stayed right there, and before long she opened one eye and squinted over the edge into the hole.

"What's the matter?" Marty asked, craning her neck to see down into the ground. "What's the matter with you, Dose?"

The lid flew off, the sand and gravel pelting her in the face, and Dose jumped to his feet, madder than he had ever been when he was living his life.

"I could wring your neck, woman!" Dose shouted at her.

"What don't please you, Dose?" Marty asked him. "Did I get too much starch in the jumper?"

"Woman," Dose said, shaking his fist at her, "you've been neglecting your duty something bad. You're stowing me away in this here ground with a pesky fly inside this here coffin. Now, you get a hump on yourself and bring me a fly swatter. If you think you can nail me up in a box with a fly inside it, you've got another think coming."

"I always do like you say, Dose," Marty said. "You just wait till I run get the swatter."

There wasn't a sound made anywhere. The shovelers didn't shovel, Hap didn't pick a note, and Goodie didn't shake a thing.

Marty got the swatter fast as she could, because she knew better than to keep Dose waiting, and handed it down to him. Dose stretched out in the splintery pine box and pulled the lid shut.

Pretty soon they could hear a stirring around down in the box.

"Swish!" the fly swatter sounded.

"Just hold on and wait," Marty said, shaking her head at the shovelers.

"Swish!" the fly swatter sounded.

"Dose got him," Marty said, straightening up. "Now shovel boys, shovel!"

The dirt and sand and gravel flew in, and the grave filled up. The preacher got his praying done, and most of the splinters out of his fingers. That banjo-playing fool, Hap Conson, started acting like he was going to pick that thing to pieces. And that behind-shaking high-yellow, Goodie, histed her dress and went misbehaving all over the place. Maybe by morning Hap and Goodie would be in their stride. Wouldn't be too sure about it, though, because the longer it took to get the pitch up, the longer it would last.

(First published in 1936 in *Mid-Week Pictorial*)

Big Buck

When the sun went down, there were a heap of people just tramping up and down the dusty road without a care in the whole wide world. It was Saturday night and the cool of the evening was coming on, and that was enough to make a lot of folks happy. There were a few old logging mules plodding along in the dust with a worried look on their faces, but they had a right to look that way, because they had worked hard in the swamp all week and suppertime had come and gone, and they were still a long way from home.

It was the best time of the whole year for colored people, because it was so hot the whites didn't stir around much, and a colored man could walk up and down in the big road as much as he wanted to. The women and girls were all dressed up in starched white dresses and bright silk hair bows, and the men had on their Sunday clothes.

All at once a hound dog somewhere down the road started barking his head off. You could look down that way, but you couldn't see anything much, because the moon hadn't come up yet. The boys stopped in the middle of the road and listened. The old dog just kept on barking. They didn't say much, but they knew good and well those old hound dogs never took the trouble to get up and bark unless it was a stranger they smelled.

"Take care yourself, nigger!" the black boy in the yellow hat yelled. "Stand back and hold your breath, because if you don't, you won't never know what hit you."

"What you talking about, anyhow?" Jimson said.

"I just turned around and looked down the road," Moses said, "and I saw a sight that'll make your eyes pop out of your head."

"What you see, nigger?" Jimson asked, trembling like a quiver bug. "You see something scary?"

"I seen Big Buck," Moses said, his voice weak and thin. "I seen him more than once, too, because I looked back twice to make sure I saw right the first time."

The two Negroes backed off the road into the ditch and pulled the bushes around them. They squatted there a while listening. Farther up the road people were laughing and singing, and talking loud. The old hound dog down the road was barking like he just wouldn't give up.

"Ain't no sense in Big Buck scaring the daylights out of folks the way he does," Jimson said. "It's a sin the way he keeps on doing it."

"Big Buck don't exactly aim to set out to scare folks," Moses said. "People just naturally get the shakes when he comes anywhere around, that's all. It ain't Big Buck's fault none. He's as gentle as a baby."

"Then how come you're sitting here, squatting in these bushes, if he ain't nothing to be scared of?"

Moses didn't say anything. They pulled the bushes back a little and looked down the road. They couldn't see much of Big Buck, because it had been dark ever since sundown; but they could hear his feet flapping in the dusty road as plain as cypress trees falling in the swamp in broad daylight.

"Maybe he once was gentle, when he was a baby himself," Jimson said. "Maybe he is now, when he's asleep in his bed. But last Saturday night down at the crossroads store he didn't act like no baby I ever knew."

"What did he do down there?" Moses asked.

"He said he liked the looks of the striped band on my new straw hat, and then he slapped me so hard on the back I hit the ground smack with my face. That's how like a baby Big Buck is. I know, I do."

"Quit your jabbering," Moses whispered. "Here he comes!"

They pulled the bushes around them and squatted closer to the ground so they wouldn't be seen. They took off their hats and ducked down as far as they could so their heads wouldn't show. They were mighty glad it had got as dark as it was.

"Just look at that courting fool," Jimson whispered. "Ain't he the biggest sport you ever did see? He's all dressed up in yellow shoes and red necktie ready to flash them colors on the first gal he sees. That courting fool can do courting where courting's never been done before. Man alive, don't I wish I was him! I'd get me a high yellow and—"

"Shut your big mouth, nigger!" Moses whispered, slamming Jimson in the ribs with his elbow. "He'll jump us here in these bushes sure, if you don't shut that big mouth of yours."

Big Buck swung up the road like his mind was made up beforehand just exactly where he was headed. He was whistling as loud as a sawmill engine at Saturday afternoon quitting time, and throwing his head back and swinging his arms like he was sitting on top of the world. He was on his way to do some courting, it was plain to see.

The colored boys in the bushes shook until their bones rattled.

Then right square in front of the bushes Big Buck stopped and looked. There wasn't no cat that could see better than him in the dark. His big black face only had to turn toward what he wanted to see, and there it was as plain as day in front of his eyes.

"You niggers is going to shake all the leaves right off them poor bushes," Big Buck said, grinning until his teeth glistened like new tombstones in the moonlight. "Why you boys want to go and do that to them pretty little trees?"

He reached an arm across the ditch and caught hold of a woolly head. He pulled his arm back into the road.

"What's your name, nigger?" he said.

"I'm Jimson, Mr. Big Buck," the colored boy said. "Just Jimson's my name."

Big Buck reached his other arm into the bushes and caught hold of another woolly head. He yanked on it until Moses came hopping out into the road. He and Jimson stood there under Big Buck's arms trembling worse than the leaves on the bushes had done.

"What's your name, black boy?" Big Buck said.

"This is little Moses," he answered.

"Little Moses how-many?"

"Just little Moses March."

"That a funny name to have in August, boy," Big Buck said, shaking him by the hair until Moses wished he'd never been born. "What you quivering like that for, boy? Ain't nothing to be scared of if you change your name to August."

"Yes, sir, Mr. Big Buck," Moses said. "I'll change it. I'll change my name just like you said. I'll do just like you told me. I sure will, Mr. Big Buck."

Big Buck turned Moses loose and laughed all over. He slapped Jimson on the back between the shoulders and, before Jimson knew what had happened, the ground rose up and smacked him square in the face. Big Buck looked down at Jimson and raised him to his feet by gripping a handful of woolly hair in his hand. He stood back and laughed some more.

"You peewees don't have to act like you is scared out of your mind," Big Buck said. "I ain't going to hurt nobody. You boys is my friends. If it wasn't so late, and if I wasn't on my way to do some courting, I'd stop a while and shoot you some craps."

He hitched up his pants and tightened up his necktie.

The boys couldn't help admiring his bright yellow shoes and red necktie that looked like a red lantern hanging around his neck.

"Which-a-way is it to Singing Sal's house from here?" he asked.

"Whoses house?" Jimson asked, his mouth hanging open. "Whoses house did you say?"

"I said Singing Sal's," Big Buck answered.

"You don't mean Singing Sal, does you, Mr. Big Buck?" Moses asked. "You couldn't mean her, because Singing Sal ain't never took no courting. She's mule-headed—"

"You heard me, peewee," Big Buck said. "I say what I mean, and I mean Singing Sal. Which-a-way does she live from here?"

"Is you fixing to court her, sure enough?" Moses asked.

"That's what I'm headed for," he said, "and I'm in a big hurry to get there. You peewees come on and show me the way to get to where that gal lives."

Jimson and Moses ran along beside him, trotting to keep up with the long strides. They went half a mile before anybody said anything.

Every time they met a knot of people in the road, the folks jumped into the ditches to let Big Buck pass. Big Buck didn't weigh more than two hundred and fifty pounds, and he wasn't much over seven feet tall, but it looked like he took up all the space there was in a road when he swung along it. The women and girls sort of giggled when he went by, but Big Buck didn't turn his head at all. He kept straight up the big road like a hound on a live trail.

It wasn't long before Jimson and Moses were puffing and blowing, and they didn't know how much longer they could keep up with Big Buck if he didn't stop soon and give them a chance to get their breath back. The folks in the road scattered like a covey of quail.

When they got to the fork in the road, Big Buck stopped and asked them which way to go.

"It's over that way, across the creek," Jimson said, breathing hard. "If you didn't have no objection, I'd like to tag along behind you the rest of the way. Me and Moses was going over that way, anyway."

I don't aim to waste no time knocking on wrong people's doors," Big Buck said, "and I want you boys to lead me straight to the place I want to go. Come on and don't waste no more time standing here."

They swung down the right-hand way. There weren't many houses down there, and they didn't lose any time. Big Buck was away out in front and the boys had a hard time keeping up.

They passed a couple of houses and went up the hill from the bridge over the creek. Big Buck started humming a little tune to himself. He didn't mind climbing a hill any more than walking on level ground.

When they got to the top, Big Buck stopped and hitched up his pants. He wiped the dust off his new yellow shoes with his pants legs, and then he tightened up the red necktie until it almost choked him.

"That's the place," Jimson said, pointing.

"Then here's where I light," Big Buck said. "Here's where I hang my hat."

He started toward the cabin through the gap in the split-rail fence. He stopped halfway and called back.

"I'm mighty much obliged to you boys," he said.

He dug down into his pants and tossed a bright dime to them. Jimson got it before it was lost in the dark.

"You boys helped me save a lot of time, and I'm mighty much obliged," he said.

"You ain't going to try to court that there Singing Sal, sure enough, is you, Mr. Big Buck?" Jimson asked. He and Moses came as far as the fence and leaned on it. "Everybody says Singing Sal won't take no courting. Some say she ain't never took not even a whiff of it. Folks have even got themselves hurt, just trying to."

"She just ain't never had the right man come along before and give it to her," Big Buck said. "I've heard all that talk about how she won't take no courting, but she'll be singing a different tune when I get through with her."

Big Buck took a few steps toward the cabin door. Moses backed off toward the road. He wasn't taking no chances, because Singing Sal had a habit of shooting off a shotgun when she didn't want to be bothered. Moses backed away. Jimson stayed where he was and tried to get Moses to come closer so they could see what happened when Big Buck started inside.

"There ain't nothing to be scared of, Moses," Jimson said. "Big Buck knows what he's doing, or he wouldn't have come all the way here like he done."

Big Buck hitched up his pants again and picked his way around the woodpile and over an old wash tub full of rusty tin cans. He put one foot on the porch step and tried it with his weight to see how solid it was. The step squeaked and swayed, but it held him up.

Out in the yard by the sagging split-rail fence Jimson and Moses hung onto a post and waited to see. When Big Buck rapped on the door, their breath was stuck tight inside of them. There wasn't time to breathe before a chair fell over backward inside the cabin. Right after that a big tin pan was knocked off a table or shelf or something, and it fell on the floor with a big racket, too. She sure had been taken by surprise.

"Who's that at my door?" Singing Sal said. "What you want, whoever you is?"

Big Buck kicked the door with one of his big yellow shoes. The whole building shook.

"Your man has done come," he said, rattling and twisting the doorknob. "Open up and let your good man inside, gal."

"Go away from here, nigger, while you is good and able," Singing Sal said. "I ain't got no time to be wasting on you, whoever you is. Now, just pick up your feet and mosey on away from my house."

"Honey," Big Buck said, getting a good grip on the knob, "I done made up my mind a long time back to start my courting while the victuals is hot. Just set me down a plate and pull me up a chair."

Before he could move an inch, a blast from Singing Sal's shotgun tore through the flimsy door. It didn't come anywhere near Big Buck, but it did sort of set him back on his heels for a minute. Then he hitched up his pants and yanked on the knob.

"Put that plaything down before you hurt yourself, honey," he shouted through the hole in the door. "Them things don't scare me one bit."

He gave the knob a jerk, and it broke off, and the lock with it. The door opened slowly, and the yellow lamplight fell across the porch and yard as far as the woodpile. He strutted inside while Singing Sal stared at him wide-eyed. Nobody had ever come through her door like that before. He acted like he wasn't scared of nothing in the world, not even double-barrel shotguns.

"Who's you?" she asked, her eyes popping.

He started grinning at her, and his whole mouth looked like it was going to split open from one ear to the other.

"I'm your man, honey," he said, "and I've come to do you some courting."

He walked on past her, looking her over from top to bottom while she stood in a daze. He walked around her to get a good look at her from behind. She didn't move an inch, she was that up in the air.

Jimson and Moses crept a little closer, going as far as the woodpile. They stayed behind it so they would have a place to dodge in case Singing Sal got hold of herself and started shooting again.

"I'm Big Buck from the far end of the swamp, honey," he said. "You must have heard of me before, because I've been around this part of the country most all my life. It's too bad I've been this long in getting here for some courting. But here I is, honey. Your good man has done come at last."

He pulled up a chair and sat down at the table. He wiped off the red-and-yellow oilcloth with his coat sleeve and reached to the cookstove for a skillet full of pout-mouthed perch. While he was getting the fish with one hand, he reached the other one over and picked up the coffeepot and poured himself a cupful. When that was done, he reached into the oven and got himself a handful of hot biscuits. All the time he was doing that, Singing Sal just stood and looked like she had just woke up out of a long sleep.

"You sure is a fine cook, honey," Big Buck said. "My, oh, my! I'd go courting every night if I could find good eating like these pout-mouthed perches and them hot biscuits."

After Big Buck had taken a bite of fish in one gulp and a whole biscuit in another, Singing Sal shook herself and reached down on the floor for the shotgun she dropped when she shot it off the first time. She brought it up and leveled it off at Big Buck and squeezed one eye shut. Big Buck cut his eyes around at her and took another big bite of perch.

"Honey, shut that door and keep the chilly night air out," he told her, pouring another cup of coffee. "I don't like to feel a draft down the back of my neck when I'm setting and eating."

Singing Sal raised one ear to hear what he was saying, and then she sighted some more down the barrel of the shotgun, but by then it was waving like she couldn't draw a bead any more. She was shaking so she couldn't hold it at all, and so she stood it on its end. After she had rested a minute, she clicked the hammer until it was uncocked, and put the shotgun back under the bed.

"Where'd you come from, anyhow?" she asked Big Buck.

"Honey, I done told you I come from back in the swamp where I cut them cypress trees all week long," he said. "If I had known how fine it is here, I wouldn't have waited for Saturday to come. I'd have gone and been here a long time back before this, honey."

He took another helping of fish and poured himself some more hot black coffee. All the biscuits were gone, the whole bread pan full. He felt on the oilcloth and tried to find some crumbs with his fingers.

Singing Sal walked behind his chair and looked him over good from head to toe. He didn't pay no attention to her at all. He didn't even say another word until he finished eating all the fried fish he wanted.

Then he pushed the table away from him, wiped his mouth, and swung a long arm around behind him. His arm caught Singing Sal around the middle and brought her up beside him. He spread open his legs and stood her between them. Then he took another good look at her from top to bottom.

"You look as good as them pout-mouthed perch and hot biscuits I done ate, honey," he said to her. "My, oh, my!"

He reached up and set her down on his lap. Then he reached out and kissed her hard on the mouth.

Singing Sal swung her nearest arm, and her hand landed square on Big Buck's face. He laughed right back at her. She swung her other arm, but her fist just bounced off his face like it had been a rubber ball.

He reached out to grab her to him, and she let go with both fists, both knees, and the iron lid cover from the top of the skillet. Big Buck went down on the floor when the iron lid hit him, and Singing Sal landed on top of him swinging both the iron lid and the iron water kettle with all her might. The kettle broke, and pieces of it flew all over the room. Big Buck pushed along the floor, and she hit him with the skillet, the coffeepot, and the top of the table. That looked like it was enough to do him in, but he still had courting on his mind. He reached out to grab her to him, and she hit him over the head with the oven door.

Singing Sal had been stirring around as busy as a cat with fur on fire, and she was out of breath. She sort of wobbled backward and rested against the foot of the bed, all undone.

She was panting and blowing, and she didn't know what to pick up next to hit him with. It looked to her like it didn't do no good to hit him at all, because things bounced off him like they would have against a brick wall. She hadn't ever seen a man like him before in all her life. She didn't know before that there was a man made like him at all.

"Honey," Big Buck said, "you sure is full of fire. You is my kind of gal to court. My, oh, my!"

He reached up and grabbed her. She didn't move much, and he tugged again. She acted like she was a post in a posthole, she was that solid when he tried to budge her. He grabbed her again, and she went down on top of him like a sack of corn. She rolled off on the floor, and her arms and legs thrashed around like she was trying to beat off bees and hornets. Big Buck got a grip on her and she rolled over on her back and lay there quiet, acting like she hadn't ever tussled with him at all. Her eyes looked up into his, and if she had been a kitten she would have purred.

"How did you like my fried fish and hot biscuits, Big Buck?" she asked, lazy and slow. "How was they, Big Buck?"

"The cooking's mighty good," he said. "I ain't never had nothing as good as that was before."

The wind blew the door almost shut. There was only a little narrow crack left. Jimson and Moses stood up and looked at the yellow lamplight shining through the crack. After that they went to the gap in the fence and made their way to the big road. Every once in a while they could hear Singing Sal laugh out loud. They sat down in the ditch and waited. There wasn't anything else they could do.

They had to wait a long time before Big Buck came out of the house. The moon had come up and moved halfway across the sky, and the dew had settled so heavy on them that they shivered as bad as if they had fallen in the creek.

They jumped up when Big Buck came stumbling over the woodpile and through the gap in the fence.

From the door of the house a long shaft of yellow lamplight shone across the yard. Singing Sal was crouched behind the door with only her head sticking out.

"What you boys hanging around here for?" Big Buck said. "Come on and get going."

They started down the hill, Big Buck striking out in front and Jimson and Moses running along beside him to keep up with him.

They were halfway down the hill, and Big Buck hadn't said a word since they left the front of the house. Jimson and Moses ran along, trying to keep up with him, so they would hear anything he said about courting Singing Sal. Any man who had gone and courted Singing Sal right in her own house ought to be full of things to say.

They hung on, hoping he would say something any minute. It wasn't so bad trying to keep up with him going downhill.

When they got to the bottom of the hill where the road crossed the creek, Big Buck stopped and turned around. He looked back up at the top of the hill where Singing Sal lived, and drew a long deep breath. Jimson and Moses crowded around him to hear if he said anything.

"Them was the finest pout-mouthed perches I ever ate in all my life," Big Buck said slowly. "My, oh, my! Them fried fish, and all them hot biscuits was the best eating I ever done. My, oh, my! That colored gal sure can cook!"

Big Buck hitched up his pants and started across the bridge. It was a long way back to the swamp, and the sun was getting ready to come up.

"My, oh, my!" he said, swinging into his stride.

Jimson and Moses ran along beside him, doing their best to keep up.

(First published in 1939 in *College Humor*)

open up that door! I reckon you must be so pinched-faced, you scared of the nighttime."

"The nighttime is one time when I ain't scared, even when you're in it, Youster Brown. Now, go yourself on off somewhere and stop worrying Sis and me."

"Old pinched-faced woman, why you scared to open the door and let me see Sis?" he asked, creeping up closer to the house.

"Because Sis is saving up for a man her worth. She can't be wasting herself on no half-Jim nigger like you. Now, go on off, Youster Brown, and leave us be."

Youster crept a little closer to the door, feeling his way up the path from the road. All he wanted was to see that door unlatch just one little inch, and he would get his way in.

"I've got a little eating-present here for Sis," he said when he got to the doorstep. He waited to hear if that old pinched-faced Matty would come close to the door. "It'll make some mighty good eating, I'm telling you."

"Don't you go bringing no white-folks' stole chickens around here, Youster Brown," she said. "I don't have nothing to do with white-folks' stole chickens, and you know I don't."

"Woman, these here ain't chickens. They ain't nothing like chickens. They ain't even got feathers on them. These here is plump rabbits I gummed in my own cotton patch."

"Lay them on the doorsill, and then back off to the big road," she said. "I wouldn't leave you get a chance to come in that door for a big white mansion on easy street, Youster Brown."

"What you got so heavy against me, Matty?" he asked her. "What's eating on you, anyhow?"

There was no sight or sound for longer than he could hold his breath. When Matty wasn't at the hearth to poke the fire, the sparks stopped coming out the chimney.

"If you so set on knowing what's the matter, you go ask Sally Lucky. She'll tell you in no time."

"Sally Lucky done give me a charm on Sis," Youster said. "I handed over and paid her three dollars and six bits only last week. I'm already sunk seven dollars in Sally Lucky, and all the good she ever done me was to say to come see Sis on every black night there was. That's why I'm standing out here now like I am, because it's a

Nine Dollars' Worth of Mumble

You couldn't see no stars, you couldn't see no moon, you couldn't see nothing much but a measly handful of sparks on the chimney spout. It was a mighty poor beginning for a courting on a ten o'clock night. Hollering didn't do a bit of good, and stomping up and down did less.

Youster swung the meal sack from his right shoulder to his left. Carrying around a couple of hobbled rabbits wasn't much fun. They kicked and they squealed, and they kept his mind from working on a way to get into that house where Sis was.

He stooped 'way down and felt around on the road for a handful of rocks. When he found enough, he pitched them at the house where they would make the most noise.

"Go away from here and stop pestering us, Youster Brown," that old pinch-faced woman said through the door. "I've got Sis right where my eyes can see her, and that's where she's going to stay. You go and get yourself away from here, Youster Brown."

"Woman," Youster shouted, "you shut your big mouth and

black night, and Sally Lucky says to come when it's like it is now."

"You go give Sally Lucky two dollars more right now, and see what happens, Youster Brown. For all that money you'll have a lot coming to you. But you won't never find out nothing standing around here. Sally Lucky'll tell you, so you'll be told for all time."

Youster laid the sack with the two hobbled rabits in it on the doorstep. Then he backed out to the road. It wasn't long before the door opened a crack, then a foot. Matty's long thin arm reached out, felt around, grabbed the mean sack, and jerked it inside. When she closed the door and latched it, the night was again as black as ever.

He waited around for a while, feeling the wind, and smelling the chimney smoke. He couldn't see why Sis had to grow up and live with an old pinched-faced woman like Matty.

When he got to thinking about Matty, he remembered what she said. He cut across the field toward Sally Lucky's. It didn't take him long when he had no time to lose. When he got to the creek, he crossed it on the log and jogged up the hollow to Sally Lucky's shack.

"Who's that?" Sally Lucky said, when he pounded on the door.

"Youster Brown," he said as loud as he could.

"What you want, Youster?"

"I want a working charm on Sis, or something bad on that old pinched-faced Matty. I done paid you seven, all told, dollars, and it ain't worked for me none yet. It's time it worked, too. If I give you two more dollars, will you make the charm work, and put something bad on Matty, too?"

The shriveled-up old Sally Lucky opened the door and stuck her head out on her thin neck. She squinted at him in the dark, and felt to see if he had a gun or knife in his pockets. She had been putting up her hair for the night, and half was up on one side of her head, and half down on the other. She looked all wore out.

"You sure look like you is the right somebody to put things on folks," Youster said, gulping and shaking. "If you is, now's the time to prove it to me. Man alive, I'm needing things on folks, if ever I did."

"Let me see your money, Youster," she said, taking him inside and sitting down in her chair on the hearth. "What kind of money you got on you?"

He took out all the money he had in the world — four half-dollar pieces — and put it on the fingers of her hand.

"I'm getting dog-tired of handing you over all my money, and not getting no action for it," Youster said. "Look here, now, woman, is you able to do things or ain't you?"

"You know Ham Beaver, don't you?"

"I reckon I know Ham. I saw him day before yesterday. What about him?"

"I gave him a charm on a yellow girl six miles down the creek, and he went and got her all for himself before the week was over."

"Maybe so," Youster said. "But I paid you seven dollars, all told, before now, for a charm on Sis, and I ain't got no sign of action for it. That old pinched-faced Matty just locks up the door and won't let me in when I want in."

"What you need is a curse on Matty," Sally Lucky said. "A curse is what you want, and for nine dollars, all told, you appear to be due one, Youster."

"It won't get me in no trouble with the law, will it?" he asked, shaking. "The law is one thing I don't want no trouble with no more at all."

"All my charms and curses are private dealings," she said, shaking her finger at him until he trembled more than ever. "As long as you do like I tell you, and keep your mouth shut, you won't have no trouble with the law. I see to that."

"I has bought charms before, and they didn't make no trouble for me. But I ain't never before in my life bought a curse on nobody. I just want to make sure I ain't going to get in no trouble with the law. I'm positive about that."

He studied the hickory-log fire for a while, and spat on an ember. He couldn't be afraid of the law as long as he had Sally Lucky on his side. And he figured nine dollars' worth was plenty to keep her on his side.

Sally Lucky picked up her poker and began sticking it into the fire. Sparks swirled in the fireplace and disappeared out of sight up the chimney. Youster watched her, sitting on the edge of his chair. He was in a big hurry, and he hoped it wouldn't take her long this time to see what she was looking for in the fire.

All at once she began to mutter to herself, saying things so fast that Youster could not understand what the words were. He got down on his hands and knees and peered into the blazing fire, trying to see with his own eyes what Sally Lucky saw. While he was looking so hard, Sally Lucky started saying things faster and faster. He knew then that she was talking to Matty, and putting the curse on her.

He was as trembly as Sally Lucky was by then. He crept so close to the fire that he could barely keep his eyes open in the heat. Then as suddenly as she had begun, Sally Lucky picked up a rusty tomato can partly filled with water, and dashed it into the fire. The water sizzled, and the logs smoked and hissed, and a sharp black face could be seen in the fire.

Youster got back on his chair and waited. Sally Lucky kept on mumbling to herself, but the double talk was dying down, and before long no sound came through her jerking lips.

"You sure must be real sure enough conjur, Sally Lucky," Youster said weakly.

She put a small tin snuff can into his hand, closing her fingers over it. He could feel that it was heavy, heavier than a can of snuff. It rattled, too, like it had been partly filled with BB shot.

Sally Lucky didn't say another thing until she took him to the door. There she pushed him outside, and said:

"Whenever you think the curse ain't working like it ought to, just take out that snuff can, Youster, and shake it a little."

"Like it was dice?"

"Just exactly like it was dice."

She shut the door and barred it.

Youster put the can into his pocket, and kept his hand in there with it so he wouldn't have a chance in the world to lose it. He ran down the creek as fast as he could, crossed it on the log, and cut across the field toward the big road where Sis and Matty lived.

There still was no light anywhere in the night. When he got closer to the house, he could see a handful of sparks come out the chimney spout every once in a while when Matty poked the hickory-log fire.

He strode up to the front door as big as a bill collector. There wasn't nothing to make him scared of that old pinched-faced Matty no more.

"Open up," he said, pounding on the door.

"That you, Youster Brown, again?" Matty said on the inside.

"I reckon it is," Youster said. "It ain't nobody else. Open this here door up, woman, before I take it off its hinges. I ain't got no time to lose."

"You sure do talk big for a half-Jim nigger, Youster Brown. Ain't you got no sense? Don't you know that big talk don't scare me none at all?"

"The talk maybe don't, but the conjur do," Youster said. "Woman, I got a curse on you."

"You is?"

"Don't you feel it none?"

"I don't feel nothing but a draft on my back."

Youster took the snuff can out of his pocket and shook it in his hand. He shook it like it was a pair of dice.

"Come on, can, do your work," he said to the snuffbox in his hand. "Get down on your knees and do your nine dollars' worth!"

While he waited for the can to put the curse into action, he listened through the door. There was no sound in there, except the occasional squeak of Matty's rocking chair on the hearth.

"I don't hear Sis in there," Youster said. "Where you at, Sis?"

"Sis is minding her own business," Matty told him. "You go on off somewhere and mind yours. Sis ain't studying about you, anyhow."

"Why ain't she?" Youster shouted. "Sis is my woman, and my woman ought to be studying about me all the time."

"You sure do talk like all the big-headed half-Jim niggers I ever knew," Matty said. "Just because you paid seven dollars to Sally Lucky for a charm on Sis, you get the notion in the head that Sis's your woman. Nigger, if I had only your sense, I wouldn't know which end to stand on."

Youster rubbed the snuffbox in his hands, feeling its slick surface and good warmth. He held his breath while he listened through the door.

"I can afford to put off getting her for a while," he said through the crack, "being as how this curse is going to be working on you."

"What curse?" Matty said.

"The curse I just a while ago got Sally Lucky to put on you for me, that's what. I paid her two dollars for it. That makes nine, all told, dollars I've paid out. All I don't feel right about is that I waited all this time before I got a curse put on you. I ought to have had it working on you all this past summer and fall."

"If you paid nine dollars to Sally Lucky for putting something on me, Youster Brown, all you got was just nine dollars' worth of mumble."

"How come?" Youster said.

"Because I paid Sally Lucky three dollars for a curse on you the first time I ever saw you, that's how come," Matty said. "And that's how come all your big talk about getting a charm on Sis and a curse on me won't never come to nothing. Charms and curses won't cross, Youster Brown, because it's the one that's taken out first that does the work, and that's how come the curse I took out on you took, and the ones you took out on Sis and me won't take. I saw you coming, Youster Brown, and I didn't lose no time taking out the curse on you."

Youster sat down on the step. He looked down the path toward the road and across the field toward Sally Lucky's. He fingered the snuff can for a while.

There came a squeak from the chair through the door, but there was no other sound. The black night was pulling down all around him. He couldn't see nothing, nowhere. There wasn't no sense in night being black like the bottom of a hole. After a while he got up and went off down the road. He was trying his best to think of some way to get his nine dollars back. Nine dollars was a lot of money to pay for mumble.

(First published in 1937 in *Harper's Bazaar*)

Meddlesome Jack

Hod Sheppard was in the kitchen eating breakfast when he heard one of the colored boys yell for him. Before he could get up and look out the window to see what the trouble was, Daisy came running into the room from the garden house in the field looking as if she had been scared out of her wits.

"Hod! Hod!" she screamed at him. "Did you hear it?"

He shook her loose from him and got up from the table. Daisy fell down on the kitchen floor, holding on to his legs with all her might.

"Hear what?" he said. "I heard one of the niggers yelling for me. That's all I heard. What's the matter with you, Daisy?"

Just then Sam, the colored boy, called Hod again louder than ever. Both Hod and Daisy ran to the back door and looked out across the field. The only thing out there they could see was the yellow broom sedge and the dead-leafed blackjack.

"What's all this fuss and racket about, anyway?" Hod said, looking at Daisy.

"I heard something, Hod," she said, trembling.

"Heard what? What did you hear?"

"I don't know what it was, but I heard it."

"What did it sound like — wind, or something?"

"It sounded like — like somebody calling me, Hod."

"Somebody calling you?"

She nodded her head, holding him tightly.

"Who's calling you! If I ever find anybody around here calling you out of the house, I'll butcher him. You'd better not let me see anybody around here after you. I'll kill him so quick—"

Sam came running around the corner of the house, his overall jumper flying out behind, and his crinkly hair jumping like a boxful of little black springs let loose. His eyes were turning white.

"Hey there, you Sam!" Hod yelled at him. "Quit your running around and come back here!"

"Sam heard him, too," Daisy said, standing beside Hod and trembling as if she would fall apart. "Sam's running away from him."

"Heard what — heard who! What's the matter with you, Daisy?"

Daisy held Hod tighter, looking out across the broom sedge. Hod pushed her away and walked out into the back yard. He stood there only a minute before the sound of Sam's pounding feet on the hard white sand grew louder and louder. Sam turned the corner of the house a second later, running even faster than he had before. His eyes were all white by that time, and it looked as if his hair had grown several inches since Hod had last seen him.

Hod reached out and caught Sam's jumper. There was a ripping sound, and Hod looked down to find that he was holding a piece of Sam's overall. Sam was around the house out of sight before Hod could yell at him to stop and come back.

"That nigger is scared of something," Hod said, looking in the doorway at Daisy.

"Sam heard him," Daisy said, trembling.

Hod ran to Daisy and put both hands on her shoulders and shook her violently.

"Heard who!" he yelled at her. "If you don't tell me who it was around here calling you, I'll choke the life out of you. Who was around here calling you? If I catch him, I'll kill him so quick—"

"You're choking me, Hod!" Daisy screamed. "Let me loose! I don't know who it was — honest to God, I don't know who it was, Hod!"

Hod released her and ran out into the yard. Sam had turned and was running down the road towards the lumber mill a mile away. The town of Folger was down there. Two stores, the post office, the lumber mill, and the bank were scorching day after day in an oval of baked clay and sand. Sam was halfway to Folger by then.

"So help me!" Daisy screamed. "There he is, Hod!"

She ran into the kitchen, slamming and bolting the door.

Out behind the barn Amos Whittle, Sam's father, was coming through the broom sedge and blackjack with his feet flying behind him so fast that they looked like the paddles on a water-mill. He had both hands gripped around the end of a rope, and the rope was being jerked by the biggest, the ugliest, and the meanest-looking jack that Hod had ever seen in his whole life. The jack was loping through the broom sedge like a hoop snake, jerking Amos from side to side as if he had been the cracker on the end of a rawhide whip.

"Head him, Mr. Hod!" Amos yelled. "Head him! Please, sir, head him!"

Hod stood looking at Amos and the jack while they loped past him. He turned and watched them with mouth agape while they made a wide circle in the broom sedge and started back towards the house and barn again.

"Head him, Mr. Hod!" Amos begged. "Please, Mr. Hod, head him!"

Hod picked up a piece of mule collar and threw it at the jack's head. The jack stopped dead in his tracks, throwing out his front feet and dragging his hind feet on the hard white sand. The animal had stopped so suddenly that Amos found himself wedged between his two hind legs.

Hod walked towards them and pulled Amos out, but Amos was up and on his feet before there was any danger of his being kicked.

"Where'd you get that jack, Amos?" Hod said.

"I don't know where I got him, but I sure wish I'd never seen him, I been all night trying to hold him, Mr. Hod. I ain't slept a wink, and my old woman's taken to the tall bushes. She and the girls heard him and they must have thought I don't know exactly what, because they went off yelling about being scared to hear a sound like that jack makes."

The jack walked leisurely over to the barn door and began eating some nubbins that Hod had dropped between the crib and the stalls. One ear stood straight up, and the other one lay flat on his neck. He was the meanest-looking jackass that had ever been in that part of the country. Hod had never seen anything like him before.

"Get him away from here, Amos," Hod said. "I don't want no jack around here."

"Mr Hod," Amos said, "I wish I could get him away somewhere where I'd never see him again. I sure wish I could accommodate you, Mr. Hod. He's the troublesomest jack I ever seen."

"Where'd you get him, Amos? What are you doing with him, anyway?"

Amos glanced at Hod, but only for a moment. He kept both eyes on the jack.

"I traded that old dollar watch of mine for him yesterday, Mr. Hod, but that jack ain't worth even four bits to me. I don't know what them things are made for, anyhow."

"I'll give you fifty cents for him," Hod said.

"You will!" Amos shouted. "Lord mercy, Mr. Hod, give it here! I'll sure be glad to get rid of that jack for four bits. He done drove my wife and grown girls crazy, and I don't know what mischief he'll be up to next. If you'll give me fifty cents for him, I'll sure be much obliged to you, Mr. Hod. I don't want to have nothing more to do with this jackass."

"I don't want him around, either," Hod said, turning to look through the kitchen window, "but I figure on making me some money with him. How old is that jack, Amos?"

"The man said he was three years old, but I don't know no way of telling a jack's age, and I don't aim to find out."

"He looks like he might be three or four. I'm going to buy him from you, Amos. I figure on making me a lot of money out of that jack. I don't know any other way to make money these days. I can't seem to get it out of the ground."

"Sure, sure, Mr. Hod. You're welcome to that jack. You're mighty much welcome to him. I don't want to have nothing more to do with no jackass. I wish now I had my watch back, but I reckon it's stopped running by now, anyhow. It was three years old, and it never did keep accurate time for me. I'll sure be tickled to get four bits for that jack, Mr. Hod."

Hod counted out fifty cents in nickels and dimes and handed the money to Amos.

"Now, you've got to help me halter that jack, Amos," Hod said. "Get yourself a good piece of stout rope. Plow line won't be no good on him."

"I don't know about haltering that Jack, Mr. Hod. Looks like to me he's never been halter broke. If it's all the same to you, Mr. Hod, I'd just as lief go on home now. I've got some stovewood to chop, and I got to—"

"Wait a minute," Hod said. "I'll get the rope to halter him with. You go in the house and wake up Shaw. He's in the bed asleep. You go in there and get him up and tell him to come out here and help us halter the jack. Ain't no sense in him sleeping all morning. I'm damned tired of seeing him do it. When he comes home, he ought to get out and help do some work about the place."

Shaw was Hod's brother who had been at home seven or eight days on leave from the Navy. He was getting ready to go back to his ship in Norfolk in a day or two. Shaw was two years younger than Hod, and only a few years older than Daisy. Daisy was nineteen then.

"I'd sure like to accommodate you, Mr. Hod," Amos said, "but the last time you sent me in to wake up Mr. Shaw, Mr. Shaw he jumped out of bed on top of me and near about twisted my neck off. He said for me never to wake him up again as long as I live. Mr. Hod, you'd better go wake up Mr. Shaw your own self."

Hod reached down and picked up a piece of stovewood. He walked toward Amos swinging the stick in his hand.

"I said go in the house and get him up," Hod told Amos again. "That sailor had better stop coming here to stay in bed half the day and be all the time telling Daisy tales."

Amos opened the kitchen door and went into the house. Hod

walked towards the barn where the jack was calmly eating red nubbins by the crib door.

When Hod reached the barnyard gate, the jack lifted his head and looked at him. He had two or three nubbins of red corn in his jaws, and he stopped chewing and crunching the grains and cobs while he looked at Hod. One of the jack's ears lay flat against the top of his head and neck, and the other one stood straight up in the air, as stiff as a cow's horn. The jack's ears were about fourteen or sixteen inches long, and they were as rigid as bones.

Hod tossed the piece of stovewood aside and walked to the opened gate for a piece of rope. He believed he could halter the jack by himself.

He started into the barnyard, but he had gone no farther than a few steps when boards began to fly off the side of the barn. The mare in the tall was kicking like a pump gun. One after the other, the boards flew off, the mare whinnied, and the jack stood listening to the pounding of the mare's hooves against the pine boards.

When Hod saw what was happening to his barn, he ran towards the jack, yelling and waving his arms and trying to get him to the leeward side of the barn.

"Howie! Howie!" he yelled at the jack.

As long as the mare got wind of the jack, nothing could make her stop kicking the boards off the barn from the inside. Hod jumped at the jack, waving his arms and shouting at him.

"Howie! Howie!"

He continued throwing up his arms to scare the jack away, but the jack just turned and looked at Hod with one ear up and one ear down.

"Howie! You ugly-looking son of a bitch! Howie!"

Hod turned around to look towards the house to see if Shaw and Amos were coming. He turned just in time to see Amos jumping out the window.

"Hey there, Amos!" Hod yelled. "Where's Shaw?"

"Mr. Shaw says he ain't going to get up till he gets ready to. Mr. Shaw cussed pretty bad and made me jump out the window."

The jack began to paw the ground. Hard clods of stableyard sand and manure flew behind him in all directions. Hod yelled at him again.

"Howie! Howie! You flop-eared bastard!"

The jack stopped and turned his head to look at Amos on the other side of the fence.

"Mr. Hod," Amos said, "if you don't mind, I'd like to have a word with you."

Hod yelled at Amos and at the jack at the same time.

"Mr. Hod," Amos said, "if I don't go home now and chop that stovewood, me and my folks won't have no dinner at all."

"Come back here!" Hod shouted at him.

Amos came as far as the gate, but he would not come any farther.

Suddenly the jack lifted his head high in the air and brayed. It sounded as if someone were blowing a trumpet in the ear.

The bray had no more than died out when the mare began pounding the boards with both hind hooves, the boards flying off the side of the barn faster than Hod could count them. He turned and looked to see what Amos was doing, and over his head he saw Daisy at the window. She looked as if she had completely lost her mind.

The jack brayed again, louder than ever, and then he leaped for the open barnyard gate. Hod threw the rope at him, but the rope missed him by six feet. The jack was through the gate and out around the house faster than Hod could yell. Amos stood as if his legs had been fence posts four feet deep in the ground.

The jack stopped at the open bedroom window, turned his head towards the house, and brayed as if he were calling all the mares in the entire county. Daisy ran to the window and looked out, and when she saw the jack no more than arm's length from her, she screamed and fell backward on the floor.

"Head him, Amos! Head him!" Hod yelled, running towards the jack.

Amos's feet were more than ever like fence posts. He was shaking like a tumbleweed, but his legs and feet were as stiff as if they had been set in concrete.

"Where in hell is that God damn sailor!" Hod yelled. "Why in hell don't he get up and help me some around here! If I had the time now, I'd go in there with a piece of cordwood and break every bone in his head. The son of a bitch comes home here on leave once a year and lays up in bed all day and stays out all night running after women. If that seagoing son of a bitch comes here again, I'll kill him!"

"Yonder goes your jack, Mr. Hod," Amos said.

Daisy stuck her head out of the window again. She was looking to see where the jack was, and she did not look at Hod. She was standing there pulling at herself, and getting more wide-eyed every second. She disappeared from sight as quickly as she had first appeared.

"Come on, you black bastard," Hod said; "let's go after him. I ought to pick up a stick and break your neck for bringing that God damn jack here to raise the devil. He's got the mare kicking down the barn, and Daisy is in there acting crazy as hell."

They started out across the broom sedge after the loping jack. The jack was headed for Folger, a mile away.

"If I ever get my hands on that jack, I'll twist his neck till it looks like a corkscrew," Hod panted, running and leaping over the yellow broom sedge. "Ain't no female safe around a sailor or a jack, and here I am running off after one, and leaving the other in the house."

They lost sight of the jackass in a short while. The beast had begun to circle the town and he was now headed down the side of the railroad tracks behind the row of Negro cabins. They soon saw him again, though, when the jack slowed down at a pasture where some horses were grazing.

A hundred yards from the cabins they had to run down into a gully. Just as they were crawling up the other side, a Negro girl suddenly appeared in front of them, springing up from nowhere. She was standing waist-high in broom sedge, and she was as naked as a pickaninny.

Hod stopped and looked at her.

"Did you see a jack?" he said to her.

"White-folks, I saw that jack, and he brayed right in my face. I just jumped up and started running. I can't sit still when I hear a jackass bray."

Hod started off again, but he stopped and came back to look at the girl.

"Put your clothes back on," he said. "You'll get raped running around in the sedge this close to town like that."

"White-captain," she said, "I ain't hard to rape. I done heard that jackass bray."

Hod turned and looked at Amos for a moment. Amos was walking around in a circle with his hands in his pockets.

"Come on," Hod told him, breaking through the broom sedge. "Let's get that jack, Amos."

They started towards the pasture where the jack had stopped. When the jack saw them coming, he turned and bolted over the railroad tracks and started jogging up the far side of the right-of-way towards Folger. Hod cut across to head him off and Amos was right behind to help.

There were very few men in town at that time of day. Several storekeepers sat on Coca-Cola crates on the sidewalk under the shade of the water-oak trees, and several men were whittling white pine and chewing tobacco. The bank was open, and RB, the cashier, was standing in the door looking out across the railroad tracks and dusty street. Down at the lumber mill, the saws whined hour after hour.

The jack slowed down and ran into the hitching yard behind the brick bank. When Hod saw that the jack had stopped, he stopped running and tried to regain his breath. Both he and Amos were panting and sweating. The August sun shone down on the dry baked clay in the oval where the town was and remained there until sunset.

Hod and Amos sat down in the shade of the depot and fanned themselves with their hats. The jack was standing calmly behind the bank, switching flies with his tail.

"Give me back my fifty cents, Amos," Hod said. "You can have that God-damn jack. I don't want him."

"I couldn't do that, Mr. Hod," Amos pleaded. "We done made the trade, and I can't break it now. You'll just have to keep that jack. He's yours now. If you want to get shed of him, go sell him to somebody else. I don't want that jack. I'd heap rather have my old dollar watch back again. I wish I'd never seen that jack in all my life. I can do without him."

Hod said nothing. He looked at the brick bank and saw RB looking out across the railroad tracks towards the stores where the men were sitting on upturned Coca-Cola crates in the water-oak shade.

"Sit here and wait," Hod said, getting up. "I've just thought of something. You sit here and keep your eyes on that jack till I come back."

"You won't be gone long, will you, Mr. Hod? I don't mind watching your animal for you, but I'd sure hate to have to look at that jack any more than I'm compelled to. He don't like my looks, and I sure don't like his. That's the ugliest-looking creature that's ever been in this country."

"Wait here till I get back," Hod said, crossing the tracks and walking towards the brick bank.

RB saw Hod coming, and he went back inside and stood behind his cashier's cage.

Hod walked in, took off his hat and leaned his arm on the little shelf in front of the cage.

"Hello, RB," he said. "It's hot today, ain't it?"

"Do you want to deposit money, or make a loan?"

Hod fanned himself and spat into the cuspidor.

"Miss it?" RB asked, trying to see through the grill.

"Not quite," Hod said.

RB spat into his own cuspidor at his feet.

"What can I do for you?" he said.

"Well, I'll tell you, RB," Hod said. "It's like this. You've got all this money here in the bank and it ain't doing you much good where it is. And here I come with all my money tied up in livestock. There ain't but one answer to that, is there?"

"When did you get some livestock, Hod?" he asked. "I didn't know you had anything but that old mare and that gray mule."

"I made a trade today," Hod said, "and now just when my money is all tied up in livestock, I find a man who's willing to let me in on a timber deal. I need fifty dollars to swing my share. There ain't no use trying to farm these days, RB. That's why I'm going in for livestock and timber."

"How many others do you own?"

"Well, I've got that mare, Ida, out there at my place, but I ain't counting her. And likewise that old mule."

"How many others do you own?"

"I purchased a high-class stud animal this morning, RB, and I paid out all my ready cash in the deal."

"A bull?"

"No, not exactly a bull, RB."

"What was it then?"

"A jackass, RB."

"A jackass!"

"That's right."

"Who in hell wants to own a jackass, Hod? I can't lend the bank's money on a jackass."

"You're in the moneylending business, RB, and I've got an animal to mortgage. What else do you want? I'm putting up my jack, and you're putting up your money. That's business, RB. That's good business."

"Yes, but suppose you force me to foreclose the mortgage — I'd have the jack, and then maybe I couldn't find a buyer. Jackass buyers are pretty scarce customers, Hod. I don't recall ever seeing one."

"Anybody would give you a hundred dollars for a good high-class jack, RB. If you knew as much about farming and stock-raising as you do about banking, you'd recognize that without me having to tell you."

"What does a jackass look like?"

"A jack don't look so good to the eye, RB, but that's not a jack's high point. When a jack brays—"

RB came running around from behind his cage and caught Hod by the arm. He was so excited that he was trembling.

"Is that what I heard last night, Hod?"

"What?"

"A jackass braying."

"Wouldn't be surprised if you did. Amos was out exercising him last night, and he said the jack brayed almost all night long."

"Come back here with me," RB said, still shaking. "I'm going to let you have that loan, and take a mortgage on that jack. I want to have a hand in it. If I'll let you have the loan, will you let me take the jack home and keep him at my house for about a week, Hod?"

"You're more than welcome to him, RB. You can keep him all the time if you want to. But why do you want to keep a jack at your house? You don't breed mules, do you?"

RB had Hod sign the papers before he replied. He then counted out five ten-dollar bills and put them into Hod's hand.

"This is just between me and you, Hod," he said. "Me and my wife haven't been on speaking terms for more than a month now. She cooks my meals and does her housework, but she's been mad at me about something and she won't say a word or have anything to do with me. But last night, sometime after midnight, we were lying there in the bed, she as far on her side as she could get without falling out, and all at once I heard the damnedest yell I ever heard in all my life. It was that jackass braying. I know now what it was, but I didn't know then. That jack was somewhere out in the sedge, and when he brayed, the first thing I knew, my wife was all over me, she was that scared, or something. That sounds like a lie, after I have told you about her not speaking to me for more than a month, and sleeping as far on her side of the bed as she could get without falling on the floor, but it's the truth if I know what the truth is. The jack brayed just once, and the first thing I knew, my wife was all over me, hugging me and begging me not to leave her. This morning she took up her old ways again, and that's why I want to stable that jack at my house for a week or two. He'll break up that streak of not talking and not having anything to do with me. That jack is what I am in need of, Hod."

Hod took the money and walked out of the bank towards the depot where Amos was.

"Where's the jack, Hod?" RB said, running after him.

"Out there behind your bank," Hod said. "You can take him home with you tonight when you close up."

Amos got up to meet Hod.

"Come on, Amos," Hod said. "We're going home."

Amos looked back over his shoulder at the jack behind the bank, watching him until he was out of sight. They walked through the broom sedge, circling the big gully, on the way home.

When they reached the front yard, Hod saw Sam sitting under a chinaberry tree. Sam got up and stood leaning against the trunk.

"What are you doing here?" Hod asked him. "What are you hanging around here for? Go on home, Sam."

Sam came forward a step, and stepped backward two.

"Miss Daisy told me to tell you something for her," Sam said, chewing the words.

"She said what?"

"Mr. Hod, Miss Daisy and Mr. Shaw went off down the road while you was chasing that jack. Mr. Shaw said he was taking Miss Daisy with him back to the navy yard, and Miss Daisy said she was going off and never coming back."

Hod went to the front porch and sat down in the shade. His feet hung over the edge of the porch, almost touching the ground.

Amos walked across the yard and sat down on the steps. He looked at Hod for several minutes before he said anything.

"Mr. Hod," he said, chewing the words worse than his son had before him, "I reckon you'd better go back to Folger and get your jack. Looks like that jack has a powerful way of fretting the womenfolks, and you'd better get him to turn one in your direction."

(First published in 1933 in *We Are the Living*)

The Courting of Susie Brown

Half an hour after the sun went down on the far side of the Mississippi, Sampson Jones was hurrying along the dusty road to Elbow Creek where Susie Brown lived all alone in her house behind the levee. Every once in a while he shifted the heavy shoe box from one arm to the other, easing the burden he was carrying.

When he jogged over the last rise of ground before reaching the levee, he saw the flickering light in Susie's window, and the sight that met his eyes made him hurry faster than ever.

Susie was inside her house, putting away the supper dishes. She was singing a little and brushing away the miller moths that swarmed around the light in the room.

Sampson rattled the rusty latch on the gate and hitched up his pants. Susie had never looked so good to him before.

"You look sweeter than a suck of sugar, baby," he shouted to her through the open window.

Susie spun around on her heels. The tin pan she was drying sailed out of her hands and clattered against the cookstove.

"What you want here again, Sampson Jones!" she cried, startled out of her wits. "What you doing down here off the high land!"

She had to stop and fan herself before she could get her breath back.

"You done found that out the first time, honey," he said, lifting the heavy shoe box and laying it before her eyes on the window sill. "Now why don't you just give up? Ain't no use spoiling it by playing you don't know why I come."

Susie studied the shoe box, wondering what it could hold. The sight of it made her hesitate. The last three times Sampson had come to court her, he had not brought her a single thing.

"I ain't got no time to waste on no sorry, measly-weight, trifling man," she said finally, turning her back on the shoe box.

"My trifling days is all over, honey," he said quickly. "I ain't trifling around no more."

Susie swung the dish towel on the line behind the cookstove and stole a quick glance at herself in the mirror over the shelf. Then she moved slowly across the room, watching Sampson and his shoe box suspiciously.

"When I get set and ready for a man, I'm going to get me a good one," she said, inspecting him disdainfully. "I ain't aiming to waste my good self on no short-weight plowboy."

Sampson grinned confidently at the scowling brown-skinned girl.

"Baby," he said, "what do you reckon I done?"

"What?" she asked, her interest mounting.

"I weighed myself at exactly two hundred and ten pounds just a little while ago previously."

He started to swing his legs through the window opening, but Susie gave him a shove that sent him dropping to the ground.

"I weigh my men on my own scales," Susie said stiffly. "I wouldn't take your weighing in any quicker than I would the next one who comes bragging along."

"What makes you think I'm lying about myself to you, honey?" he asked unhappily. "Why you crave to go and talk like that?"

"Because you don't weigh nowhere near two hundred pounds, that's why," she said sharply. "I done made up my mind over the kind of man I want when I get myself ready to want him, and you ain't the one I'm thinking about. It don't make no difference at all what you brings me in a shoe box, neither." She paused for a moment, getting her breath. "You hear what I say, Sampson Jones?"

"I hear you, honey," he said. "But it would make me downright awful sad if you was to make a bad mistake for yourself."

Susie leaned out the window and stared down at the box under his arm.

"Maybe if you was to find out what I brung you," he said, "you'd swing around to the other kind of talk. I sure has got a pretty thing for you, honey. I brung it all the way from Mr. Bob Bell's store at the big crossroads."

Susie glanced at the box, and then she straightened up and looked Sampson all over from head to toe. The white shoe box was tied tightly with heavy yellow twine. It gleamed enticingly before her eyes in the moonlight, only an arm's length away.

"How much you say you really sure enough weigh?" she asked, continuing to look him up and down.

"I done told you two hundred ten, honey," he said hopefully. "Why you think I ain't telling you the whole lawful truth?"

Sampson watched her for a while, wondering if she were going to believe him this time. He had been coming down from the high land to see her for six months, trying his best every minute of the time he was there to court her into marrying him. Sometimes he succeeded in getting his arms around her for a little while, hugging her some around the waist and a little around the neck, but usually she kept him at a distance by making him stay outside on the ground while she sat on the porch, talking to him through the window.

No matter how well he argued with her, Susie had always said that the man she was going to take up with had to weigh two hundred pounds, or better. Sampson had never weighed more than a hundred and sixty pounds in his whole life, until he began courting her. Now he had managed to put on thirty additional pounds in six months' time after eating all the beans and fat pork he could put his hands on. But during the past month he had discovered that no matter how much he ate, he was not able to increase his weight a single pound over one hundred and ninety.

And to make matters worse, his worry over that was causing him to lose weight every day. He had become desperate.

While he was standing there on the ground outside her window, Susie had moved away. Sampson hurried around to the front of the house. Susie had seated herself on the rocker on the porch, and she was sitting there placidly fanning her face.

Sampson set one foot on the bottom step hopefully.

"Don't you dare come one single more inch, Sampson Jones!" Susie said sharply. "I ain't satisfied in my mind with the weighing you said you done to yourself."

Sampson patted his expanded stomach and slapped his heavy thighs with his great brown hands.

"Woman," he said crossly, "you sure is one aggravating creature. Here I is with all this man-sized weight on my frame, and you act like you don't even see it at all. What's the matter with you, anyhow?"

He slammed the shoe box on the second step from the bottom, threw out his chest and thrust out his arms to show his bulging muscles.

"Why don't you get some scales and let me weigh you then, if you're all that sure?" she said. "You ain't scared to let me weigh you in, is you?"

Sampson stopped and thought it over carefully. After a while, he looked up at Susie.

"I'd be tickled to have you weigh me in, Susie," he said, "only I ain't got no scales to do it on. Has you?"

Before she could reply, he stooped down quickly and picked up the heavy shoe box.

"Drop that box, Sampson Jones!" she said sharply. "I know what you're up to. You're trying to trick me with that heavy box you've got there."

"No, I ain't, Susie," he said, startled. Sheepishly he put the box down on the step. "What makes you think a sorry thing like that about me?"

"Well," Susie said, rocking some more, "if you ain't lying in your talk, maybe you'll weigh in on my stillyerd."

Sampson's face fell.

"Has you got a stillyerd here, Susie, sure enough?"

Susie stood up.

"You stand right where you is now, and I'll bring it," she told him. "I'm getting all tired out from hearing all your boasting. The weighing in will settle it." She moved toward the door. "That is, if you ain't scared to show me your true weight."

"I ain't scared one bit, Susie," he said fearfully.

When she had gone out of sight into the house, Sampson ran out into the yard and began picking up all the rocks and stones he could put his hands on. He filled both hip pockets with the largest ones, and then began scooping up fistfuls of gravel and filling all his other pockets. Susie still had not returned, and so he hastily untied his shoes and stuffed them with all the sand he could get into them. He straightened up, trembling all over, when he heard Susie come toward him through the house. He was certain he had not succeeded in loading himself with the necessary ten pounds of stone, sand, and gravel. At the last moment, he found another stone and put it into his mouth.

Susie brought the weighing steelyard to the porch and hung it on a rafter. Then she looked around for Sampson.

Sampson went up the steps carrying the heavy shoe box under one arm. He thrust his other arm through the loop of rope dangling from the steelyard.

"Set the box on the floor," she ordered firmly.

He looked at her, pleadingly, for a few moments, but recognizing the determined expression on Susie's face, he dropped it.

"I been plowing hard all day in the cotton field, from sunrise to sunset," he began. "I wouldn't be taken back at all if I'd lost a heap of pounds, Susie."

"We'll see," she said harshly. "Hitch yourself up on that still-yerd."

Sampson thrust his arm through the loop and painfully swung himself clear of the floor. While he hung there, knowing his fate was in the balance, Susie stepped over and slid the weighing ball along the steel arm.

He tried to twist his head back in order to watch the weighing, but he was in such a cramped position that it was impossible for him to see anything overhead. He gave up and hung there by one arm, praying with every breath.

By the time Susie had satisfied herself that her weighing of him was accurate, Sampson was dizzy from strain and worry. He barely knew what he was doing when he heard Susie's voice tell him to set himself on his feet.

When his feet touched the floor, his knees began to sag, and he found himself staggering across the porch. He reached the wall and dug his fingernails into the rough weatherboarding in an effort to find support. Susie still had not said anything since she told him to get down from the steelyard, and he was too weak to ask her anything about it.

Presently he felt Susie's arms around his neck. The next moment he felt himself sliding downward to the floor.

When he regained his senses, Susie was kneeling beside him, hugging him with all her might. He struggled free of her grip and got his breath back. The stone he had been holding in his mouth was gone. He could not tell whether it had fallen out, or whether he had swallowed it. He was uneasy.

"Honey," Susie was saying to him, "I sure am happy about the big way you weighed in. Looks like you'd have done it for me sooner, instead of waiting all this long time."

"How much did I weigh in at, Susie?" he asked.

"Honey, you weighed exactly two hundred and fifteen pounds," she said delightedly. "And only a little while ago you said it was only two-ten. My, oh, my!"

Sampson closed his eyes.

When he looked up again, he saw Susie busily opening the heavy shoe box. She untied the string and took off the lid. Then she lifted out the ten-pound sadiron he had brought her with the hope that when he weighed for her he would be able to keep the box under his arm.

"It's the finest present I ever had in all my life, honey," she said sweetly, running the palm of her hand over the smooth surface.

She gazed at him admiringly.

While he waited for her to speak again, he glanced quickly up into her face, wondering how he was going to be able to rid himself of twenty-five pounds of stone before she discovered it on him.

(First published in 1941 in *Coronet*)

Squire Dinwiddy

My wife and I moved to the country toward the end of June, hopefully looking forward to a long restful summer in the Connecticut hills. But we soon discovered that we had been overly optimistic. It seemed that we were too far back in the hills to interest maids, housemen, or even tree surgeons. Nobody from the agencies wanted to work that distance from Stamford or Bridgeport.

We had been doing our own housework for a week when we looked up one morning while cooking breakfast to see a big shiny black limousine drive up and stop. A Negro man about thirty years old and wearing what appeared to be the remnants of a ragbag after it had been picked over came around to the kitchen door and knocked lightly.

"Good morning, boss," he said, peering through the door. "How you folks making out?"

My wife was all for sending him away without more ado, but by that time he had opened the screen door and had stepped into the kitchen.

"Good morning," I replied civilly. "Lost?"

"No, sir, boss," he said, his lips rolling back from two neat rows of the whitest teeth I had ever seen. "I'm right here. I ain't lost one bit."

"What do you want?" my wife asked him.

"I'se come to take hold," he said.

"Take hold of what?" I asked, concerned.

"Take hold the work, boss," he answered, grinning.

"Who sent you?" my wife and I asked simultaneously.

"Nobody sent me," he said. "I just heard about it and come."

My wife and I looked at each other, each wondering if the other were going to be able to think of something to say. Our attention was drawn back to the Negro when he opened the screen door and shooed a stray fly out of the kitchen.

"What can you do?" my wife asked at last.

"Anything you or the boss wants done, Missy," he said respectfully. "Eating, drinking, clotheses, driving, laundering — anything at all. Now, you folks just go sit down in comfort at the table and make yourself feel at ease, and I'll have your breakfast in front of you in no time at all. I'll fix up my extra special omelette and see how you folks take to it."

We moved toward the dining room.

"How much do you want in wages?" I asked.

"Would it hurt you to pay fifteen a week, boss?"

"Well," I said hesitatingly, "maybe we can stand it."

"I'll take thirteen and a half," he said almost obligingly, "if that'll help you out any."

We backed through the door.

"What's your name?" my wife asked.

"Squire," he said, grinning until his white teeth gleamed from ear to ear. "Squire Dinwiddy."

When my wife and I reached the hall, we stopped and looked at each other questioningly for a moment. All we could do was to nod our heads.

"Squire," I called through the door, "now that you've got a new job, don't you think you ought to return that limousine to your former employer —"

"Boss," he spoke up proudly, "that there's my machine. I'se the lawful solitary owner."

We backed carefully into the dining room, watching our step.

All went well until one morning about a week later. It happened to be the Fourth of July. My wife and I had been out late the evening before, and at seven o'clock we were sound asleep. But not for long. There was a terrific explosion on the lawn just outside our window. I rushed from bed, threw open the screen, and looked out. There squatted Squire Dinwiddy, holding a lighted match under the fuse of the biggest firecracker I had ever seen. The fuse began to spew, and Squire dashed away and got behind a tree. The salute went off, charring the grass and blowing a hole in the earth. My wife screamed.

"Squire!" I yelled. "What are you doing?"

Squire stuck his head cautiously around the trunk of the tree and looked up at me in the window.

"It's the Fourth of July, boss," he said, grinning happily. "Did you forget all about that?"

"No, I didn't forget," I said. "And it's not up to you to remind me at this time of morning, either."

"I still got one more to shoot off, boss," Squire said, striking a match and setting the fuse on another giant cracker to spewing.

"Hold your ears!" I shouted to my wife just in time.

The cracker went off while Squire was still running from it. When the report sounded, it caught him by surprise, and he jumped two feet off the ground. Then he stopped and looked around.

"It makes celebrating best when they go off when you ain't expecting them to, don't it, boss?" he said, grinning up at the window.

"Maybe," I said.

Three weeks later, just when we had accustomed ourselves to Squire's manner of running the house, he came in one morning and said he was sorry to have to do it, but that he had to go away for several days on a business trip.

We were upset by his sudden announcement, and my wife protested vigorously.

"Can't you postpone your trip for a while, Squire?" she said.

"We can't get anybody to take your place on such short notice."

"I'm sorry about the notice I didn't give," Squire said apologetically, "but the time crept up on me while I wasn't paying attention."

"At least," my wife said, "you can wait a day or two. Maybe by then we —"

"No, ma'am!" he said, emphatically, "I just naturally can't wait. I'se got to be in Washington by six o'clock this very day."

"Six o'clock!" I said. "How do you expect to get to Washington by six o'clock!"

"On the plane, boss," he said. "I'se flying down on the two o'clock plane from New York."

My wife and I looked at each other helplessly.

"That costs a lot of money, Squire," she said, hoping to discourage him. "Do you realize what it costs?"

"Yes, ma'am," Squire said, "but I add it to my expenses."

"What expenses?" I asked. "What expenses are you talking about?"

"The expenses of doing business," Squire said.

My wife and I stared at each other bewilderedly.

"What kind of business?" I asked, wondering.

"I kind of forgot to mention it to you, I reckon," Squire said sheepishly. "I has to go to Washington once every month to collect the rents."

"What rents?" I asked. "Whose rents?"

"My rents," he answered. "I'se got twenty-seven families living in my tenements down there, and I can't afford to let the rents fall behind: The rents just can't be collected, not in Washington, noway, if you let them run over. Because the renters will let you get an eviction against them, and after that they have the law on their side. They don't have to pay the past-due rent at all after that. So that's why I never let the renters get that far along. I stay just one jump ahead of what they're thinking in their heads down there while I'm up here."

My wife and I could only stare at Squire for a long time after he had finished. He began to grin then, his lips rolling back from his straight white teeth.

"Why, that makes you an absentee landlord, Squire," I said

finally, shaking my head.

"It sure does, boss," he said, his whole face agrin. "That's why I'm taking the plane this afternoon. I don't aim to be absent when the rents come due. No, sir, boss!"

Squire bowed, backing toward his shiny black limousine with the silver speaking tube. He grinned broadly as he got in and started the motor. As he rolled away, he stuck an arm out and waved to us.

"Good-by, boss!" he called. "I'll be right back again as soon as I collect the rents!"

We raised our arms and waved until he was out of sight. After that we turned and stared at each other, wondering what there was to say.

(First published in 1941 in *Esquire*)